BAR NONE

By: John Coleman

First print 2017 June

This is a book of fiction. Any references or similarities to actual events, real people, or real locations are intended to give the novel a sense of reality. Any similarity to other names, characters, places and incidents are entirely coincidental.

ISBN: 9781693709043

Cover Design: Crystell Publications

Book Productions: Crystell Publications
You're The Publisher, We're Your Legs
We Help You Self Publish Your Book
(405) 414-3991
www.crystellpublications.com

DEDICATION

IF YOU HAVE ONE, SEND THIS TYPED IN CORRLINKS.COM

John Coleman

ACKNOWLEDGEMENTS

IF YOU HAVE ONE, SEND THIS TYPED IN
CORRLINKS.COM

PROLOGUE

"If you think you're grown and can't follow the rules of my house then you can get out." Jilla's mother told him.

At the young age of fourteen, Jilla took to the mean streets of Chicago. The minimum wage job that Jilla's mom worked didn't pay enough for her to satisfy the expensive taste of clothing that Jilla developed at a young age, nor was it able to give him the large sums of money that he saw the neighborhood drug dealers flaunt on a regular basis. Jilla wanted that for himself so when he walked out the door of his mother's house, Jilla never looked back.

"Aye Big Bubba!" Jilla shouted catching Big Bubba coming out of the liquor store.

Everybody knew Big Bubba and knew to stay away from him once he'd drank too much. At 19 years old he stood 6' 3" and weighed 313 pounds. Big Bubba always kept a 40 ounce of Old English in his hand, and when he got sloppy drunk he loved to beat people up.

"What up lil bad ass Jilla? What you doing outside this late? Yo' ole G gone be creeping around in a minute. You know you s'pose to be in the crib, the street lights on."

"Man I need to stay at your crib tonight."

"Again! Your lil ass run away more than any mufucka I know" Big Bubba said cracking open his 40 ounce. "It's all good though lil homie. You know I got you. Just come on through when you get ready. I'll be down in my room."

Big Bubba's was always a reliable place for Jilla to lay his head whenever he left home. That was one thing that he loved about Big Bubba, the big fella always held him down when he needed it.

* * * *

Later that night, after Jilla was done shooting dice at Murda Park', and beating them out of $350, he went and bought a couple of dime bags of weed from Cook's spot then headed to Big Bubba's house. Jilla couldn't ring the doorbell because if Big Bubba's mother would have found out that he was harboring Jilla it would 've been hell to tell the captain. Luckily Big Bubba's room was in the basement so Jilla just used the secret knock they'd made up.

Tap, tap. Tap, tap, tap. Tap, tap.

Knowing it was Jilla, Big Bubba went to the back door and let him in. "What's the deal young fool?"

"Shit big homie, just got through breaking them niggaz at 'Murda Park'. They was sweet as hell tonight." Jilla responded pulling a bunch of crumpled up money out of his pocket.

Tossing the weed over to Big Bubba, he began rolling the blunts as Jilla straightened out and counted his winnings. Jilla loved counting dead Presidents. It gave him the rush of all rushes and he knew that they would always get him all the cars, clothes, jewelry and hoes that a young nigga could want.

"Shorty, I see you keep a lil bankroll in them pockets." Big Bubba said as he fired up the blunt,

"I should've came up there and got me some of that money if it was that sweet. Cause you know I got the rawest shot in the hood."

"Naw, big homie, you got the *second* rawest shot in the hood. I'm the man on this land." Jilla prided himself.

"Aye Great. Great!" Hollered, Big Bubba as he was standing outside of Great's apartment building. He and Jilla were walking through the projects located behind the Jeffery Manor.

"Big muthafuckin' Bubba." A dark-skinned dude with a low haircut shouted with his head stuck out of a 4th floor apartment window. "Hold on fool, I'm about to come down there and holler at you."

Seconds later, the infamous GREAT bombarded his way through the crowd of fiends lined up to buy cocaine from his crack spot. It was the first of the month, so the line was very long. So long in fact that it was coming outside of the building.

Great was the epitome of a hustler/gangster. He had the entire East-Side of Chicago sewed up on the cocaine and he stayed on some gangster shit no matter where he was. Jilla couldn't believe Big Bubba was turning him on to Great. But hey, Big Bubba must know that real recognize real, Jilla told himself.

"What's the deal Big Bubba?" Great asked, looking him up and down, happy to see him. "I ain't seen you in a minute."

"1 just been chillin' Great. I got me a lightweight job, downtown shining shoes. Mom's been on me so hard lately, I had to do something to get her out of my ear. I been hearing so much venom spat on your name though, a mufucka had to come back here and check you out. Plus, I got somebody I want you to meet."

As Great and Big Bubba were walking and talking, Jilla stayed quiet and kept his eyes wandering around with his finger on the trigger of his .380 automatic. He had won it from a burglary specialist kid named Cool Fingers, shooting jump shots. Ever since he'd won it, Jilla kept it on him 24/7.

Great stayed on so much bullshit that Jilla knew he had to be on point. It was no telling when somebody might get the courage to try to get back at Great for some snake stunt that he had pulled.

"What you mean mufuckas been spitting venom on my name? You know nobody want it with the G.R.E.A.T. It's kill the baby, sell the blood with me." Great said, showing Big Bubba his .45.

"You know I know the business with you Great. I be creeping with ole girl Angie though, Speedy's girl. She was telling me how you, Luke, and Rello had kicked in they door and stuck 'em for a few bricks, some green, and about $60, 000. She said, the only way they got found was that y'all left the door cracked on the way out and some church people came by the next morning. She said, if they wouldn't have been trying to get some donations for some shit, they wouldn't have been able to hear them screaming through the duct tape."

As they were talking, Jilla noticed two guys walking suspiciously towards them with hoodies on holding their heads down. He figured he was just tripping though. *It's probably just some closet smoking mufuckas not wanting nobody to see they faces*, he thought to himself. The next thing he knew, those same two guys, who he knew were suspect, had him, Great, and Big Bubba laid down on the ground at gunpoint.

"You thought it was over? You thought it was sweet like that? Geno, search 'em. Bitch ass Great either about to take me to my shit, or he about to get a 'great' bullet in his muthafuckin' head."

Now that they were up close, with their hoodies off, Jilla could see who they were. It was the dude Speedy who Great and em' had stuck up, and one of his homeboys named Geno. Jilla was familiar with them from seeing them around the hood.

Speedy had a 9-millimeter Ruger with a 30-round clip hanging from it, aimed at Great, and Geno had his beamed down on Big Bubba. By Jilla being a shorty, they made the mistake of not paying him any attention.

Geno placed his pistol in his waistline and began searching Great. He disarmed him of his .45 Smith & Wesson and placed it in the back pocket of his jeans. As he and Speedy focused on searching Big Bubba and Great, Jilla eased his hand into his pant's pocket and gripped the trigger of his .380.

Ain't no way I'm about to let these soft ass dudes get off on us, Jilla thought to himself. As soon as Geno started searching Big Bubba, Jilla eased his pistol out of his pocket. Firing off two rounds, he shot Speedy in the forehead. Seeing Speedy's lifeless body falling to the ground, and Geno turning toward him reaching for the gun tucked inside his waistline, Jilla shot him twice in the chest and three times in the face.

After Geno's body fell, Great and Big Bubba sprung up off the ground and hurried over to where the guns had fallen down. As they picked them up, Jilla stood there breathing hard and staring at the two bodies that he'd just deadened.

"Come on young fool. We out of here." Great hollered.

Taking off to the back road of the projects, they all jumped in Great's Benz and he skirted off.

It was then, with Jilla's first set of bodies, that Great took a liking to him and took him under his wing.

John Coleman

CHAPTER ONE

Awakened by the banging on the front door, Red looked over at the clock on the wall. "Jilla get up, It's your shift. Get the damn door." she screamed, from inside the bedroom.

"Aight, I got it." Jilla replied, as he groggily made his way to the door wiping cold out of his eyes.

"What up, Smitty?"

"Damn Jilla, I been knocking on the door for about 20 minutes now. What type of operation y'all running that y'all can't even answer the door?"

"My bad, Smitty. I was knocked out man. We was up all-night last night. Plus Colors fell asleep without waking me up for my shift. What you need though?"

"Let me get six for $100.

"Aight, here you go Smitty." Jilla said, handing him the six $20 bags of crack out of a sandwich bag full of them.

"You lucky I like you.

"Alright Jilla. If it's fire, like it usually be, I'll be back in about an hour.

"I'll see you in an hour then, Smitty. Don't smoke all that shit in one place either."

After securing and locking the door, Jilla headed back into the living room. "Damn Red, why you ain't just serve that chump for me?"

"Boy I'm tired. I been out all motherfuckin' night in stilettos and you think I give a fuck about answering a damn door?

"Yeah okay, I bet you if Great was here you would've broken your neck to answer that door."

"Oh well, too bad Great ain't here, huh? Now I guess you gotta do what you get paid to do."

Red was Great's prostitute, Jilla heard him say on a many a day, 'Dope money is for sho' money, but ain't no money like hoe money.' Red had to have had some bomb ass head or some killer pussy because she brought home at least $3000 a night. Red was a dime piece; 5'5", the complexion of a white girl, long black curly hair that came down to the middle of her back, a face like Angelina Jolie, and a body like Beyoncé. Red kept a belly ring in the navel of her flawless stomach, and her hair, nails, and toes stayed freshly done. Nobody in the world could've guessed that she was a hooker. She looked like the type that any man would wife. Not Great though. He worked her like a Hebrew slave.

As Jilla searched through the channels until he found SportsCenter, he grabbed half of the blunt that was left in the ashtray from the night before, He lit it up, took a pull off it, and looked around the room at the two guys that he viewed and carried as his brothers. They were knocked out, sleeping like babies.

Lil Dusty was asleep in the Lazy Boy. At the young age of eleven Lil Dusty could steal a car in 2.2 seconds, shoot dice like he came out of the womb doing it, sold more drugs than the neighborhood pharmacy, and did not have the slightest problem with busting a cap in a motherfucker's ass. With two younger sisters, two younger brothers, a mother on drugs, and a father nowhere to be found, Lil Dusty had to learn how to put food on the table early, and by any means necessary.

Over on the couch was Colors. Colors was Jilla's guy even before he'd started kicking it in the projects. Jilla brought him back there with him because he knew Great would admire his dedication to the hustle. Colors' grew up in a single parent household as well. Instead of his father dying before his birth (like Jilla's), Colors' dad walked out on his mother while she was in the hospital giving birth. He was chasing a heroin habit then, and still to this day he's still chasing that same high and hasn't returned home.

We all know that it's a struggle for a woman to raise a man. With that said, there they were; Jilla, Dusty, Colors, and Red, all living in a crack house together, chasing that paper.

Jilla took another drag from the blunt and someone knocked on the door again. "What up Mary?"

"Hey… Jilla, with your cute little black self. Let me get three of 'em."

"Aight, let me see your money first though, Mary. Your daughter Trina tried to give us a phony twenty-dollar bill yesterday.

"Boy, here! You can look at my money. I ain't never played them types of games with y'all. I ain't got nothing to do with what Trina do."

"Aight, calm down Mary." Jilla said as he held the twenty dollar bill up to the light in search of the strip that was supposed to be going through it. "It's all good. As a matter of fact, here goes a lil something extra for you. Don't say I ain't never gave you shit. Tell Trina I'mma let Lil Dusty loose on her ass the next time she tries to pull a stunt."

By Lil Dusty being so young, he played a lot and was always giving his customers a hard time. Great got on him time and time again about chasing the customers away, but it never seemed to work. Eventually Great just gave up and came to realize that Lil Dusty was going to be, Lil Dusty.

Jilla served the other six customers that were in line behind Mary then shut and locked the door. He went to continue watching SportsCenter while counting the money.

The spot was juking half a kilo a day in bags. Jilla was responsible for a half a kilo, and Colors and Dusty were responsible for nine ounces apiece. Great always appointed Jilla the heaviest task no matter what the assignment was. He consistently told him that he was the future.

13, 14, 15, 16...... Jilla had $16,000 all laid out evenly in thousand-dollar stacks, eight hundred odd dollars, plus about six more ounces left. Before they'd fallen asleep the night before, Colors and Dusty had each given him $10,800 apiece. It was already in the safe. Jilla then placed the $16,000 that he had, in the safe as well, and then pocketed the odd $800. *37,600 down, and $5,600 to go,* Jilla thought to himself. *That'll be made within the next few hours and I'll be ready for Great.* That was Jilla's procedure every day and he had it down like clockwork.

CHAPTER TWO

The money was coming in hard. Great had Jilla in charge of all finances and was even allowing him to hang out with the crew. Jilla was only 15 years old at this point and he was kicking it in clubs and after hour joints like he was grown. The first night that Great took Jilla out with him was also the first night that Jilla actually got to meet Luke and Rello on an up close and personal kicking it level. He had always seen them riding around the hood in their luxury cars, and heard about the major moves they were making, but he had only dreamt about the day he might actually be within their circle. They were the neighborhood superstars.

Great and Jilla walked into the East of the Ryan. East of the Ryan was a popular after hours joint where people could enjoy the nightlife after all the other clubs were closed for the evening. Great, Luke and Rello hung out there every night until it was time for them to pick their hoes up. Most of the guys there were hustlers and most of the women there were looking for a hustler to pay 'em and lay 'em.

"Great is in da building!" Announced the security man at the door.

He allowed him and Jilla to pass right by him unsearched. They got that treatment every time they went out.

They were always the only ones inside the place with guns. "What's the deal Lucky? I see you got the house packed as usual. You gone have to start cuttin' yo' boy in on some of this big cash you makin'. You gettin' way too much money up in this joint." Spat Great.

Lucky was the owner of East of the Ryan. He was an O.G. who put in about a year's worth of hustling after he got out of the joint from doing a 13-year bid. He saved up enough money to buy him a nightclub and a few more businesses so he could call it quits. Lucky had enough self-discipline to not get caught up in the allure of the game, something that not too many people can do. He was not only street smart; he was business savvy as well. "Naw my nigga, I'm just tryin' to catch up with you."

Sizing lil Jilla up, Lucky looked up at Great with questioning eyes

"Shorty with you?"

"Yeah, he the future. He all good."

"Aight my nigga. Luke and Rello over there at the bar. I got to move around and make sure my people on their jobs like they supposed to be. Go ahead and do you my main man. Enjoy yourself. Make yourself at home and *please* don't make my janitor have to clean up no blood tonight." Lucky said as he gave Great some dap. "Nice meeting you too young buck." he said to Jilla.

Turning around and making it through the crowd, Lucky mingled with and greeted all of his patrons. His charm often proved to be one of the main attractions of his establishment.

Jilla and Great headed to the bar where Luke and Rello were. "Heeyy Great!" shouted a mocha complexioned lady eying him with that *come and get me* look.

"How you doing sweetheart?" Great responded, as nonchalantly as ever.

He never let a female get the upper hand on him. Everywhere he went, beautiful women would flirt and come on to him from all directions. Most of them simply got ignored until he got ready to play with them.

"What's the deal my niggas?" Great greeted Luke and Rello as he approached them.

Great rarely smiled but almost every time he was around Luke and Rello he was happy and his face showed it. Great had mad love for his guys.

"Short stakes, bad breaks; stick up, rob, and take." answered Luke.

Luke and Great had been homies ever since their juvenile days. It wasn't too much that they hadn't done together.

"Pimpin' ain't dead, them hoes just scared." Rello replied.

He was the oldest out of the three. He'd taught Great and Luke a lot of what they knew.

"I want y'all to meet my lil nigga, Jilla." Great said as Jilla stood there nervous, but never showing it.

"This the young fool that offed that bitch ass nigga Speedy and his pussy ass flunky Geno?" asked Luke.

"Yeah, this my lil Go-getter."

"Shorty, I hear you wicked with them hammers. I like that

lil killer. That mean I'm gone have to keep my eyes on you, huh?" Rello said, as he tapped the long ash off of his Newport cigarette and dumped it into the ashtray and took down the last swig of his Miller Genuine Draft. "Just remember that killing is a crime and murder is a mystery."

Rello was always known for quoting some strategic shit that from books he'd read while in prison. One thing Jilla came to learn though, none of it was ever a lie.

"Well Young Jilla, you rolling with the big boys tonight.

"What you drinking?" Great asked, as he pulled a roll of money out of his pocket and motioned for the bartender to come over.

"I'm good, Great. You know I don't drink, that alcohol shit is nasty. I'll just take a bottled water."

"Ain't nothing wrong with that lil nigga.

Great, Luke, and Rello all drank, smoked weed, and snorted cocaine. Jilla didn't do anything but smoke weed. All of them extra highs, he wasn't into.

"Let me get a bottle of water for my lil man, a double shot of Martell fo' the O.G. Rello, two double shots of Hennessy for me and Luke, and three long neck Miller Genuine Drafts."

After the bartender delivered the order, Great, Luke, and Rello got to parleying, chopping it up.

Jilla noticed a dice game going on in the corner so he went over to see if he could hit a quick lick. He had about $1,500 on him. He had brought a portion of his savings with him since he knew he'd be hanging with the big boys. $1,500 should be enough to skin these old cats, he thought to himself. He knew they'd take him lightly, being a youngster and all.

For about ten minutes, Jilla just watched as the dice made their way around the circle. After a short while of observance, he felt as none of the old heads could match his shot. Feeling confident, he jumped inside of the circle and anxiously awaited his turn.

There were about eight people total in the dice game. Jilla guestimated that it was somewhere around $45,000 that he could win. He licked his chops at accomplishing that feat. This was, by far, the biggest crap game he'd ever been in.

The dice finally made it around to where Jilla was in the circle. All the old heads were eager to fade him. Just like Jilla figured, they were sweet. They looked at him like a piece of cotton candy as well. That wouldn't last long though. Jilla passed on them old fools about twenty times in a row.

It don't get no sweeter than this, Jilla thought to himself. About thirty minutes went by and Jilla was still on the dice. He was hot and couldn't miss a point. He was hitting everything. Jilla had won about $14,000 and now was working with a total of $15,500 after he had finally fallen off.

About three people after him, the dice had gotten to a light skinned dude. He had just shown up because Jilla hadn't seen him in the circle before. When the dice got to the light skinned dude, he switched them to a different color. He had brought his own dice. Some people didn't like shooting with certain colored dice because they felt that it was bad luck. Jilla personally didn't care what color dice he shot with because he felt that he won off of skills, not luck.

Switching the white dice with some red ones, the light skinned dude got to hitting point after point, like Jilla did. His point kept being six or eight, or he'd hit a seven or eleven out of the door. Everybody who faded him kept getting struck. He passed so many times, everybody had become nervous to fade him. Right then and there, Jilla knew the winner of the crap game was going to be between two people, him and light skinned dude.

Since everyone else was nervous, Jilla began fading him. Where he came from, you had to have heart to have money. Jilla wasn't scared to fade nobody. As Jilla faded him, light skinned dude continued hitting point after point. Before Jilla knew it, he'd lost all his money. Jilla wasn't going out like that though.

Going over to the bar, Jilla asked Great to loan him some money until they got back to the spot. "Man, young fool, what they over there striking you like that?" Great asked him.

"It's some light skinned, Rico Suave looking mufucka over there hitting like never before. Don't trip though, I got him as soon as I touch the dice again."

Handing lil Jilla a knot of money, folded up in a rubber band, Great gave Jilla $3,000 "Here you go lil nigga. You better come up with that."

Finding his way over to the crap game again, Jilla waited on his turn to come back around. Once it did, Jilla jumped back down and did his thang. He won the money he'd lost back, plus $16,000 more before he fell off. Now he was back.

The dice made their way back to the light skinned dude again. Sweat dripping from his head, he forcefully threw down $2, 000 and said he wasn't shooting nothing less than that. Everybody in the circle either became scared to bet, or didn't have the money to fade him, so Jilla matched the bet. The light skinned dude got on the dice and passed fourteen times in a row, nothing but sevens or elevens. He struck Jilla for everything. Jilla couldn't believe it.

Walking back over to the bar, Jilla was heated. "What happened lil homie? Don't tell me they got you again." questioned Luke.

As Jilla was explaining how Light Skinned dude had heated up on him, a Lisa Raye looking chick walked up on Great and whispered something into his ear. The fellas thought she was on some freaky shit but Great jumped up and yelled, "What!!!"

Come to find out, light skinned dude's name was Yella Boy. He was better known as Y.B and he had been using Tees in the dice game against Jilla. Tees, are dice loaded with magnets in the middle of them. The magnets make whoever's shooting them hit certain points all the time.

Great slammed his beer bottle down on the bar, pulled out his pistol, and marched towards Y.B., who was now sitting at a table talking to some chick. Luke, Rello and Jilla pulled out their pistols as well and followed suit. Walking up to Y.B., Great grabbed him by his ponytail and stuck his pistol in his mouth. "Let's go, I need to talk to you."

Great led Y.B. out the side door of the club, which led to the alley, and threw him up against the wall. Luke, Rello, and Jilla all had their pistols aimed right at Y.B.'s face with nothing but murder in their eyes.

"You been cheatin' my lil homie, bitch ass nigga?" Great hollered, looking like he was about to blow Y.B.'s face off.

"Naw Great, I didn't know he was with you. I swear man."

Y.B. pled with the fear of God in his voice.

"I guess you should've known then pussy Mufucka. Cause now you about to pay for not being aware of your surroundings."

When Great said that, Jilla thought he was giving him the green light to start putting holes inside of Y.B. He immediately cocked the hammer of the Ruger he'd taken from Speedy that day when he murked him and Geno. Great stopped him in his tracks. "Slow down lil gunslinger. We gone have some fun with this shiesty mufucka."

While all of this was going on, Luke and Rello were busying themselves taking all of Y.B.'s money and jewelry. Luke was unclamping and unscrewing the jewels, and Rello was emptying the pockets. After Luke and Rello were done cleaning him out, Great had a devilish grin on his face.

"Today just might be your lucky day. I guess beating mufucka on the dice is yo' hustle and I can't knock the hustle. However, there comes a price for not being aware of your surroundings. I can't allow you, or no other mufucka, to get away with trying me or anybody else on my team so I'm gone give you two alternatives. Either you strip buck naked right now, or I'm gone give my trigger happy lil nigga, Jilla here, the okay to start Swiss cheesing yo' ass. I'm quite sure he would love to do that right about now, so which one is it gone be?"

Jilla was hoping that Y.B. didn't comply, because he was more than heated once he'd found out that he'd got gotten over on.

Immediately, Y.B. got to unbuttoning and unbuckling all his clothes. Within 30 seconds he was completely naked. Great gathered up everything that he had taken off and dumped it in the sewer.

As Y.B.'s clothes were floating away, Great said, "I guess you gotta figure out how you getting home now playboy."

Walking away, everyone was laughing. Rello turned around and said, "You lucky I ain't got time to fuck your pretty ass.

They all laughed even louder as they left Y.B. standing there in the alley just like that. He was left all alone with nothing. No clothes, no phone, no car keys, no money, no nothing. Feeling as humiliated as ever.

Great, Luke, Rello, and Jilla split up into two groups. Luke and Rello jumped into Luke's BMW, while Jilla and Great got into Great's Mercedes Benz. It was time to go pick the Hoes up. On the way out west, Great got to lecturing Jilla about how Y.B. had gotten over on him. "Man, lil Jilla." he said, steering the car with his knee as he used a matchbook cover to scoop one on ones of cocaine into his nostrils, out of an eight ball that he had in a plastic sandwich bag. "Out here in these streets. *Sniff, sniff.* Niggaz got more moves than ex-lax. *Sniff, sniff.* You got to always keep yo' eyes on everybody, cuz somebody always got they eyes on you. *Sniff. sniff.* That goes from the President to a bum livin' on the streets. *Sniff. sniff.* Everybody got a hustle."

Great always tried to make sure that Jilla learned from his mistakes. With Jilla's father dying a week before he was born, Great assumed that he was the father figure Jilla was always deprived of.

CHAPTER THREE

"Jilla." a voice whispered as he walked through the projects, on his way to get some Philly Blunts from the corner store.

Jilla looked around to see who it was but didn't notice anyone trying to get his attention. He figured he was just blowed as hell from the Purple Haze that him, Dusty, and Colors had just got done smoking, so he kept on walking.

"Jilla." whispered the voice again.

He quickly turned around in the direction that the whisper came from and caught a head trying to unnoticeably duck back behind a tree. Jilla palmed the 9-millimeter that was tucked inside his waistline, keeping it concealed beneath the white t-shirt he was wearing, and walked towards the tree. As he got close, he pulled the gun out, no longer concealing it, and cocked the hammer. His heart was beating faster and faster the closer he got to the tree. When he finally reached it, his finger gripped the trigger, ready to execute and, *BAM*!!!

What he saw caught him by complete surprise. It was a girl. She was blushing with an ear to ear smile and chipped tooth, looking as innocent as ever. Jilla quickly tucked his heat back into his waist and looked around, hoping no one had seen what had just gone down. Luckily, no one had observed.

The chipped tooth girl was one of the many young females who'd developed a crush on young Jilla. He often found himself wondering if she'd ever realized how close she came to death trying to gain his attention.

"Shorty what's wrong with you? Is you crazy? You damn near got shot playin' them games." Jilla said to the girl as he checked her out looking her up and down.

The girl was caramel complexioned, thick like a young stallion, and had a round pretty face. Her hair, shoes and clothes were roughed up, but with minor repair, she could definitely be a head turner.

"Hee, hee, hee, hee." she giggled in response, not uttering a word.

She just held her head down acting as shy as ever.

"Well what's your name? It ain't fair that you know mine and I don't know yours?" Jilla asked trying to pry.

"Camelle." she answered, head still down, finally, peeping up only to bat her eyelashes.

Jilla persuaded her to walk to the store with him while he continued to get to know her. Camelle turned out to be his first lil chick. Her shyness didn't last long though and she ended up taking Jilla for a hell of a ride.

CHAPTER FOUR

Great and Jilla were sitting in front of Shakers, waiting on the hoes to come out. Luke and Rello were parked behind them in Luke's car.

Shakers was a strip club owned by a guy named Gus who Rello knew from prison. Due to how they had gotten jammed, while incarcerated, Gus allowed Rello, Jilla, and Luke to bring the girls there every night, free of charge.

As they waited, Great was on the phone with Lynn, his main chick, telling her that he would be home in a little while. Jilla was just laid back, listening to the Scarface that Great had playing, and zoning off the blunt that they'd just took to the head.

After about 15 minutes went by, out came the hoes, Passion and Strawberry, who were Luke and Rello's girls. They jumped in the back seat of Rello's car. Red jumped in the back seat of Great's ride. Great was a true pimp. He never allowed any of his niggaz to get in the back seat for no female, unless it was Lynn. She was the only one with Wifey status. Immediately after Red jumped in the car, she handed Great a balled-up knot of money and he instantly began counting it.

"Bitch! This all you got?" Great shouted, counting it again to make sure he hadn't miscounted. "How the fuck you only got fifteen hundred dollars?" he yelled like he was about to kill her.

Before they dropped Red off for work, earlier that night, she was complaining to Great about not wanting to go in because she'd just found out that she was pregnant with his child. Great told her that he didn't give a fuck, that the baby wasn't his, and that she was going to sell pussy until the water bag busted.

"I told you I didn't feel good tonight baby. I've been throwing up and everything. But I was still able to make that money there for you." Red responded, hoping it would save her from what she knew was about to come.

As soon as she said that, Great slammed on the brakes, jumped out of the car, and snatched Red out the back seat like she was a ragdoll. He started beating her like she was a slave, a male slave at that. Red was hollering and screaming for her life, begging Great to stop. Her whole body went numb from the pain she was suffering. Everywhere except her stomach. As she lay on the ground, motionless and covered in blood, she balled up in the fetal position, knowing she had probably just lost the baby.

"Jilla, pop the trunk." Great hollered, out of breath.

Jilla opened the glove compartment and pushed the button to pop the trunk. Great picked Red up, threw her in the trunk, shut it, and hopped back in the car. Luke and Rello were pulled over laughing the whole time, while Passion and Strawberry were staring with tear filled eyes. They both had been through what Red was experiencing on numerous occasions. Red had to ride all the way back to the spot in the trunk. Alone, with nothing to think about except what happens when you come up short on a pimp's money.

As they were driving, Great turned down the music and said, "Never let a hoe get out on you Young Jilla. If you give an inch, she gone think you soft and try to take a mile. You gotta keep the fear of God instilled in a hoe. Always remember that."

Once they got back to the hood, Luke and Rello went their separate ways and Great dropped off Jilla and Red at the spot. While Jilla ran upstairs to grab Great's money, Great had let Red out the trunk and was talking with her. When Jilla came back down, Great sent Red upstairs and let Jilla know where to find the next brick that he had stashed in the spot. Great then left and Jilla headed upstairs to chop up the work with Dusty and Colors.

CHAPTER FIVE

"Man fool, Camelle got some weed." Colors frantically said to Jilla, while showing him a $40 bag of weed.

"Where she at?" Jilla responded, shouting from the window to Colors who was standing on the sidewalk.

"Here she come walking this way now." responded Colors with his back turned toward Camelle and her friend Tanya, so they wouldn't know he was talking about them.

Jilla ran out the front door of the spot and flew down the stairs, careful not to scuff up the new pair of Jordan 6's he had on. They still had the orange and white plastic tag hanging off them, with the Jordan logo floating through the air. Jilla kept the tag on to advertise to everyone that his kicks were fresh out the box.

Colors and Jilla stood in front of the building until Camelle and Tanya made their way to where they were. Once they did, Jilla grabbed Camelle by her hair and started pulling her toward the spot. "Stoppp." Camelle whined, trying to pry Jilla's fingers from her hair.

"Bring yo' mufuckin' ass here." Jilla said as he led her up the stairs, never loosening his grip. "What you got for me?"

"What are you talking about Jilla?" she replied, playing stupid.

Jilla got her in the spot and began searching her pockets but didn't find anything. He then began searching her bra and BINGO! He found a sandwich bag filled with weed.

As he pulled it out of her bra, all Camelle did was smile. She'd put it there on purpose just to get Jilla to feel on her.

"Where you get dis shit from?" Jilla asked while looking at the weed. He was thinking about how him, Colors, and Dusty were going to have a smoke fest with it.

"My cousin Kim's house."

"Where she get it from?" Jilla then asked, trying to see if it was more where it had come from.

"Her boyfriend be having all types of stuff over there. I be finding it when I'm babysitting for her."

Camelle's cousin, Kim, was a gold-digging type of female. She was pretty and she knew it. She utilized her beauty well to manipulate money getting dudes into taking care of her. Jilla wasn't mad at her though. He was always taught, if you see a sucker lick his head.

"What's her boyfriend's name? Jilla questioned Camelle trying to see if he knew him.

"Shotgun." she informed him, raising a red flag in his head.

Shotgun the dude who hangs at the East of The Ryan all the time, Jilla thought to himself. The reason he recognized the name was because he'd heard Great, Luke and Rello scoping out and plotting on him for a minute. The only problem was, he always had a crew of guys with him everywhere he went. The man was rumored to be worth over a million dollars. He had the whole wild hundreds on lock with weed, cocaine, and heroine.

"How much more of dis shit do he got up in her crib?" Jilla asked hoping that this was his chance to hit the jackpot. He was anticipating the opportunity to show Great and them that he could get down just like them.

"I don't know. It be different amounts at different times when I go over there."

"Well, when the next time you goin' over there to babysit?"

"I don't know. Whenever she calls me and says she need me to." Camelle answered.

"Aight, so when you go back over there, you gone let me stick him?"

"Boyy no!!! You know that's my cousin's boyfriend." Camelle blurted out looking wide eyed. "I can't do that. Anybody else but my family Jilla."

When Camelle said that, Jilla couldn't even say anything in response. He just took her in the room, peeled off her clothes like he knew she wanted him to, and sexed her real good. Camelle had begun to love the way it felt when Jilla pushed in and out of her. She felt feelings rush through her body that took her to a whole other place every time he did.

Jilla had to reward her in some type of way for bringing him the weed. One thing that Jilla knew for sure was that he had broken Camelle's virginity and she loved him. As he pleased her, he got a nut off, but was simultaneously trying to figure out how he was going to get her to let him stick up Shotgun.

CHAPTER SIX

Great was on Lake Shore Drive heading home. He stayed downtown, in a condo overlooking Lake Michigan, with Lynn. As he wove in and out of traffic, his eyes stayed planted on the rearview mirrors. It was a habit. As much dirt as he'd done, it was a must that he remained security conscious.

Exiting at Michigan Avenue, Great observed the headlights of the same black Impala he'd been suspecting of following him ever since he'd jumped on Lake Shore, exiting as well. Seeing that the light up ahead of him was red, Great hit his left blinker and switched over to the left turning lane. While waiting for the light to turn green, he had his left hand on the wood grain of the steering wheel and his right hand planted on the automatic Uzi that was on his lap. The black Impala was three cars behind his attempting to go unnoticed. Great was the king of the rearview mirror so he noticed.

As soon as the light turned green, Great punched it and made a quick right turn shooting pass the other three lanes of cars that were to the right of him, heading in the same direction as he was. None of the other vehicles had even gotten a chance to move. After a helluva traffic maneuver, and a few honks from disgruntled drivers, Great had shook whoever it was that was following him. He bent a few more corners and finally arrived at his place of residence.

Being the extra cautious individual that he was, Great circled the block three times more checking for followers. Satisfied, he pulled into the underground parking garage of the twenty-story building. He parked, jumped out of the car, and popped the trunk. After grabbing the three duffel bags of money, full of his day's earnings, he shut the trunk back and headed to the elevator. Once inside the elevator, all that he could think about was who could it have been that was following him.

Entering his apartment, Great dropped the duffel bags on the plush carpet floor and kicked off his shoes. He could smell the aroma of the vanilla scented candles that Lynn had been burning, as he made his way to the bedroom. When he entered the room. she was laid across the bed asleep. He could tell that she'd tried to wait up for him due to the black laced Victoria Secret negligée that was wrapped around her body. It looked as if it had been painted on. The matching black high heeled shoes, with the fuzzy ball on the fronts, were on the floor next to the bed. As he stood there staring at her sleeping, he flashed back thinking about all the women he'd had throughout his lifetime. Hypnotized by her beauty, he could now see why none of the others had managed to grow on him the way she did.

Great had met her while he was in the hospital one of the six times that he'd been shot. She was working a job as a nursing assistant so that she could pay her way through college. Lynn was going to school to become a neurosurgeon.

When she first walked into his hospital room, it was love at first sight for Great. The nursing uniform she sported had fit her 5'8", 160lb frame to perfection. She was all thickness and beauty. After indulging in several conversations with her, Great came to learn that she was classy but also had that hood in her. They clicked on all cylinders and he made it his business to sweep her off her feet from that day on.

After admiring his sleeping beauty, Great began to awake Lynn with nothing but wet kisses. Starting at her forehead, he kissed his way down to her right ear. As his tongue meticulously twirled around inside her earlobe Lynn awoke with a faint moan of approval. Great then made his way down to her neck. Lynn's breathing became heavier and heavier. This was her spot and Great knew it. From her neck he descended down to the perfections of her 36B breasts. Lynn had the type that every woman wanted. Great sucked and licked on them with stellar skill, causing her eraser sized nipples to stiffen and become as sensitive as ever. Licking his way down the flatness of her stomach, he made a trail to her toned right leg. As he lifted it off the bed, and into the air, he sucked each one of her freshly manicured toes one by one. Great sent shivers of delight throughout her entire body like a shockwave.

"Damn baby!! What are you doing to me?" Lynn purred. Great sat her right leg down and repeated the same service to her left set of toes. Lynn's body shuttered intensely. Great loved to make Lynn cum. To him it was the best sight in the world. Making his way up her left leg, Great now focused on her inner thigh. He teasingly licked around her Brazilian waxed love box causing her moans to grow louder and louder. "Oooh baaaby... don't stop baby damn that feels so good." she moaned.

Grabbing the back of Great's head, Lynn led his face to where she so desperately wanted his lips to meet. Great obliged and navigated his tongue around her clit taking Lynn over the brink of another climax.

After cumming three more times Lynn pled, "Give it to me baby. I need to feel you inside me. Pleeaase give it to me."

She needed to feel Great pulsating while sliding in and out of her. It had been close to a week since he'd last been home so she couldn't wait to be filled with his thickness.

Six positions later, and after they both were drenched in sweat, Lynn fell asleep in Great's arms. She loved the way he made her cum. No one had ever even come close to doing it better. While she was cuddled up under Great, his mind was working overtime. He kept trying to figure out who it was that was following him.

Sliding his arm slowly from underneath Lynn's neck, Great left her sleeping soundly in the bedroom and went into the living room to count the money he had in the duffel bags. It was time for him to re-up. The only thing I'm waiting on now is for Luke and Rello to get through, he thought to himself. Great grabbed his phone and dialed Rello's number.

"What up, G?" Rello answered half asleep.

"Man fool, I'm ready to go holla at Flaco tomorrow. I'm just waiting on y'all." Great told him.

"Aight. We got one of our mans lined up to come holla at us from Joliet in the morning; to grab these last two. We'll be ready for you right after that." replied Rello.

"Aight my nigga. Just hit me when y'all get through with them then."

"In the morning my nigga."

"In the morning."

CHAPTER SEVEN

"Happy birthday Jilla!" Everyone shouted in unison as Jilla walked into the fieldhouse of Trumbull Park.

Colors, Dusty and his guys from the front part of the hood had thrown him a surprise party for his 17th birthday. Colors had told Jilla that they were supposed to be meeting a gun connect who had some bullet proof vests for sale.

Music was blaring through the speakers and everyone from the front to the back of the hood was in attendance. The girls were bunched up in little cliques and so were the guys.

Dressed in their best outfits, the girls were all hoping to catch the eye of young Jilla. Most of the guys there highly respected Jilla and his comrades. Some were there just to stalk their girls, making sure they weren't picking or choosing. Then you had the few that were hard core haters. Dudes always had their eyes on Jilla because he was more advanced amongst the peers of his age range. His game was always about five years sharper.

Jilla, Colors, and Dusty all walked through the crowds

shaking up and giving daps to the fellas, while getting hugs and lust-filled stares from the girls. Jilla didn't do the party thing too much because all the young tenders that he was sexing would all be under the same roof at the same time. He knew that couldn't help but lead to some type of confrontation.

Even though Jilla consistently instructed the girls that he messed with not to ever front him off in public, there was always that one rebel. She was the one who wanted the status that came along with being with Jilla so bad, that she was willing to take an ass whooping to get it.

Jilla, Colors, and Dusty navigated through the crowd over to where their guys Demon, Slim, and Ugly were. They were Luke and Rello's little go-getters and they held it down for the front of the hood. When all six of them got together, weaklings didn't want to be anywhere in sight.

"Jilla what's the deal killer?" Demon greeted while giving Jilla a gangster hug. "Happy B-Day my nigga, " He finished while handing Jilla a gallon of Hennessy.

"Plus, we got plenty of swisher wraps." Slim cut in.

"And an ounce of the purp." Ugly said while holding up a sandwich bag full of dro' and sporting an ear to ear smile.

Even though it wasn't officially Jilla's birthday until midnight, him and his future family were about to get fucked up and bring his 17th birthday in in style.

While Jilla and his guys were rolling up the dro' and sipping on Cognac, Dusty, being the playful lil dude that he was, ran around the party harassing the girls by feeling them up and pulling their hair. He was bad as hell and the chicks hated to see him coming. Especially when he had that dro' in his system.

Jilla didn't mind it though. As long as his lil guy was happy and with a smile on his face, he could care less about how somebody else felt. Especially some chick.

As they continued smoking and drinking, Jilla kept his eyes on Dusty because if anyone harmed or endangered him in any way, Jilla would bring the wrath of God upon them. After taking another sip of the Hennessy, Jilla passed it to Colors. Slim passed Jilla a dro' blunt at the same time. Taking a puff of it, Jilla noticed some girl bending down, pointing in Dusty's face, and hollering at him because he'd snatched one of her friends' ponytail weave out of her hair. The mystery girl who was hollering at Dusty was an eyecatcher and Jilla wondered to himself why he'd never seen her before.

"Who is that over there talking to Lil Dusty?" Jilla asked Demon while pointing in the direction of the most beautiful girl he'd ever seen in his life.

"That's his cousin, Destiny." Demon responded.

"How come I ain't never seen her before? She ain't from around here or somethin'? Did she just move around here?"

"Nah, she a schoolgirl. She don't hardly come outside. I'm surprised her mother let her come here tonight."

"Who she fuckin' wit'?" Jilla further prodded, even though it didn't matter.

He already knew it wouldn't be long before she belonged to him, despite who she messed with.

"Nobody that I know of. I told you she a schoolgirl G. she stuck up as hell. Everybody in the front done tried to holler at her. She don't give nobody no action though."

When Demon told him that, it made Jilla all the more

determined to make her his. "It's only two things I ain't never seen before my nigga." Jilla said, with a sly grin on his face.

"And what's that?" Demon asked, knowing Jilla had something slick he was about to say.

"A U. F.O. and a hoe that won't go." Jilla quipped.

They both started laughing and Jilla handed Demon the blunt that he'd had in his hand. They then made their way over to where Destiny and her friends were.

Destiny and the girls she was with all looked like the nerdy schoolgirl type who wouldn't seem to be into street hustling guys like Jilla and his crew. At least all of them except for Demon's sister, Michelle. Jilla used to catch her creeping with Colors all the time. If Demon would've found out, that would've been Michelle's ass. Michelle hung with them because Destiny's Grandmother lived down the street from her and they'd been best friends since kindergarten. Jilla still couldn't figure out how he'd never seen her and Destiny together before.

"Dusty what you doin' over here messin' with these girls? You don't even know them." Jilla said knowing all the time that Destiny was his cousin.

"Yes, I do fool. This my cousin."

"Yeah." Jilla responded, admiring the closer view he was able to get of Destiny.

"My name Jilla. How you doing sweetheart?" he asked, looking into Destiny's spellbinding brown eyes.

"Fine." she responded, sending off a slight attitude.

"I asked you how you doing, not how you look." Jilla spat

back, feeling as if he had to pull out some of his best lines.

When he said that, Destiny' s attitude reciprocated into one with a welcoming smile. Once he got her blushing Jilla knew his magic was working.

"Come on Lil Dusty, we over here." Jilla said in an attempt to relieve Destiny and her friends from his terrorist like acts.

Jilla didn't want to pour it on too thick, so he figured him and the guys would make their way back over to the corner of the room where they'd been chilling,

"Alright shorty, hopefully I'll be seeing you around." Jilla said as him, Demon and Dusty began to walk off.

"My name ain't shorty." Destiny responded, resurfacing her attitude.

"I know Miss Destiny." Jilla stated, catching her by surprise.

With a puzzled look on her face, Destiny asked, "How you know my name? I don't remember telling you."

"It ain't too much that go on in the Jeffery Manor that I don't know about." Jilla answered walking off, looking over his shoulder, flashing a Colgate smile.

He felt he had laid his mack game down strong. To just be turning seventeen, he had more game than the hall of fame. The killing part about it, was that he knew it.

As the night progressed, Jilla found himself not able to keep his eyes off Destiny. It had to be at least 50 girls in attendance and not one of them even came close to comparing to her beauty.

Admiring Destiny from a distance, Jilla was interrupted by

a tap on his shoulder. "Man fool, look who just came in the door." Said Ugly.

It was Camelle and her girls. They walked through the door like they just knew they were the shit. They had on matching blue Girbaud outfits, with brand new navy & baby blue Air Max gym shoes. They all had their hair and nails done as well.

Jilla was hoping that Camelle didn't come over to where he was and try to front him off. Everyone already knew that she was his girl, but he still felt that it wasn't any need for her to be all up on him. Especially with Destiny on location. He figured that Camelle had only made her way to the party for two reasons. One, to stalk him and two, to try and outshine the rest of the girls.

R. Kelly's, *Bump and Grind* came on and as people rushed to the dance floor, so did Camelle. Moving her body methodically to the music, she stared Jilla down. Swaying from side to side and rolling her hips like a professional belly dancer, Camelle stole the show. All of the boys were watching her, in awe, but her performance was meant for one set of eyes only, Jilla's.

After the show was over, so was the party. Everybody was outside heading their separate ways, going home. Jilla spotted Destiny and her girls getting ready to leave as well and had Demon call Michelle over to where they were. Handing a piece of paper to Michelle with his name and number on it, Jilla told her to give it to Destiny.

Leaving and catching back up with her girls, Michelle

handed Destiny the piece of paper. Destiny then turned around looking at Jilla and he waved goodbye to her.

"Nigga I know your bitch ass ain't just give that hoe your number." Camelle said, coming from out of nowhere. She had been stalking from a distance and Jilla hadn't even peeped her.

"What you just call me?" Jilla asked.

"You heard what I said. Your pussy ass always tryin' to fuck with some bit—."

Before she could finish her sentence, Jilla slapped her so hard that it sounded like a gunshot.

Camelle took off running and Jilla chased her down. When he finally caught her, he beat her up some more and made her repeatedly apologize to him in front of the crowd of onlookers. After he was finally done, Camelle got up, clothes all dirty and bloody, reached inside of her pocket, and threw something at him.

After she took off running again, towards the projects, Jilla picked up what she had thrown. It turned out to be an ounce of cocaine tied up in a plastic sandwich bag.

After realizing what it was that she'd thrown at him, Jilla tucked it inside of his pocket and took off running after her again. When he finally found her, she was inside of one of the project hallways crying like a lout puppy.

Jilla took Camelle upstairs to the spot and sexed her down. Making her good in that fashion always had gotten him back on her good side. After making her feel better, it was interrogation time.

Putting his pants back on, Jilla began questioning Camelle. "Where you get this shit from?" he asked, throwing the ball of cocaine on the bed.

"From my cousin's house." she replied, laying in the bed with the covers pulled over her. "I just took a little bit out so me, Tanya, and Cheri could get us some outfits for the party."

"That nigga be having cocaine over there too?"

"Yeah, it be money and guns too sometimes.

"So you be taking this shit and they don't even be missing it?" Jilla prodded, trying to estimate just how much stuff Shotgun actually left over there.

"Naw, they don't even be knowing. It be a lot." With that said, Jilla became more determined to get Shotgun. He had to figure out where Kim stayed at.

CHAPTER EIGHT

This is channel 9 news broadcasting live from 79th and Stoney Island. After a high-speed chase and police shootout, four men are dead and one is wounded. Luke F. Anderson died from multiple gunshot wounds attained from the Chicago Police department. Two officers were killed, and one has been critically wounded as a result of the shootout as well. All officers' names shall remain anonymous at this time. Also, the body of Rello S. Jenkins was pulled out of the passenger seat of the Dodge Charger, which was wrapped around a light pole as a result of the police chase. He was rushed to Stroger Hospital, by way of ambulance, and announced dead on arrival. This seems to have been a drug related matter. Two kilograms of cocaine and $60,000 were located by the C. P. D., inside the trunk of the car. There were also two automatic weapons found. No further details have been disclosed at this moment. We'll be sure to keep you updated as we learn more. This is Jerry Moore *from Channel 9, signing off.*

Great was sick to his stomach. He couldn't believe what he was seeing, or hearing. All he could do was sit and stare at the television in shock. He had just lost out on $100,000 plus his two niggaz who he would go against anybody on this whole entire earth for. Both had just been taken away from him by the strong arm of the law. Only this time it wouldn't be for some years or some months, it would be forever.

"Baby are you okay?" Lynn asked, looking at her man knowing that he wasn't feeling anything right now but hurt and pain.

Great didn't respond. He just threw the remote control on the coffee table in front of him, sat back on the couch, and massaged his temples with the tips of his fingers. Lynn then rubbed her hand on his leg and attempted to pull his dick out to suck on it and make him feel better in a way that she knew she always could. Great simply pushed her hand away. He'd never refused a head job from Lynn before. She knew he was really hurting when he did that. She decided she'd better just go into the room and let him have some space to sulk in peace. At that moment it seemed to be all he needed.

After Lynn went into the bedroom, Great looked up at the spot where he'd thrown the remote control, wondering what he was going to do, now that his two niggaz were gone. He noticed a piece of mail, sticking out from a pile of bills, addressed to him from the Federal Bureau of Prisons, Terre Haute USP. He grabbed it and opened it up. It was from his guy Quick Draw.

"G,

What's the deal my nigga? I hope shit is all good out there with y'all. I don't know if you heard or not, but your boy might just be about to touch back down in a minute. Yeah that's right, the beast is subject to be released. You know they couldn't hold the kid down for long. I got action on my appeal, so they granted me a retrial. Keep your fingers crossed for me. I can't wait to see you niggaz again. I'm counting down, and before you know it, it's going to be on like Donkey Kong again. Make sure you have the strippers and the bottles ready.

Luv My Nigga,

"Q.D."

With all of the bad news Great had been bombarded with, this was much needed good news. Quick Draw was the fourth member of Great's four-man team. He had got caught up on a murder case involving his parole officer. So Great, Luke and Rello had been paying an attorney to fight the case on appeal for him. Even though they felt they were appealing on a limb, due to the murder happening in front of three eyewitnesses, they still had their determination to keep fighting. Great knew that Quick Draw would see the news about Luke and Rello in the pen. He also knew that he had to have been feeling the same pain that he was feeling right now as well. He was expecting to receive another letter from him in the next couple of days.

Powering his phone back on, Great called up Luke's and

Rello's mothers. He had turned it off because as soon as the news coverage had hit the air, his phone began blowing up. He informed their moms that he shared their grief and that they didn't have to worry about the payments for their funerals, he'd take care of them.

Great then jumped into the shower and got dressed. On the way out of the door he instructed Lynn to call Gatling's Funeral home and set up the funeral arrangements.

Everybody who was somebody had their funeral services at Gatling's. To Great, his two guys were top notch, so he was going to make sure they had top notch funerals.

* * * * *

Ring... Ring... Ring...

"What's the deal my nigga Y.B.? I know you heard about your boys, Luke and Rello." asked Mo, as he sat in the parking lot of Harold's Chicken smacking on some chicken gizzards.

"Yeah, I just got through seein' them bitch ass boys on the news. Fuck them chumps. That ain't gone do shit but make what we got to do all the sweeter." retorted Y.B.

"No question fool. As a matter of fact, you know they funerals gone be within' the next week or two. So the best time for it to go down is right after he bury his boys." Mo said, while at the same time picking a piece of meat from between his teeth with a toothpick.

"Yep, yep, I'm feelin' that." Y.B. said with a wide grin on his face. "It ain't gone be no fun when the rabbit get the gun."

He had been patiently waiting for the time to come around

so he could get some get-back for the shit Great and them had pulled on him that night at the East of the Ryan. That was the most humiliating day of his life.

Mo wanted to get at Great and them immediately after the shit had happened but, Y.B. being more of a planner/ thinker, insisted that they wait a minute so that they wouldn't be prime suspects. He figured that Great and them stayed on so much underhanded shit that they'd eventually pull some type of move on somebody else. That would be the perfect opportunity for the microscope to be pointed in some other direction when Homicide got to doing their investigation

Y.B. never anticipated on things falling this sweet for him, but his patience ended up paying in more ways than one. Unbeknownst to Great, Y.B. had really been doing his homework on him. He had even managed to find out where Great laid his head. He had dedicated a many of days and nights following him and Lynn. Mapping out their every move with nothing but vengeance on his mind. It wouldn't be long now. The get-back was near.

Aight Y.B. I'm about to head over to Bally's and get me a workout right quick." Mo said, starting up his Ford Mustang. "Plus, it's this thick lil thang that work at the counter that I been tryin' to nail for a minute now. She be playin' hard to get but you know yo' boy gone handle that. I'm gone hit you up after I come up outta there. It' s supposed to be a big crap game up at the car wash on Cottage Grove tonight. You know we got to go through and break that motherfucker."

"Aight fool. I'm bout' to get on up and throw on some clothes so I can make a few moves myself. I'll link up with you in a minute my nigga. Be safe."

Mo headed to Bally's with the plan weighing heavily on his mind and Y.B. jumped in the shower with the same thing weighing just as heavy on his. All that both of them kept thinking was, Payback is a motherfucker.

****

Great, Jila, Dusty, and Colors were singing along with Tupac's, *Life Goes On*, as they drank Hennessy and smoked blunts, mourning the deaths of Luke and Rello. As many as times as they'd heard the song, they'd never felt it as much as they were feeling it now.

Red entered into the living room to bring the guys the burgers and fries that Great had her cook for them. As they were zoning out to Pac, and satisfying their munchies, Great's phone vibrated letting him know that he had a message. He sat his burger down, flipped the phone open, and began to read.

My friend, I hear what happened to your associates. I send my condolences. However, business is business and it is time that I see you. I need for you to meet me at the restaurant tonight. I will be leaving the country on a business trip in the morning, so it is critical that we meet tonight. You will need to show up by nine and, as always, please don't be late. 2:57 A.M.

Besides the deaths of Luke and Rello, another thing that had Great's mind turning was paying Flaco. The $100,000 that he had lost out on when Luke and Rello got killed, plus the $10,

000 he had to spend toward their funerals after they got killed, had really hit him hard. Due to his excessive spending habits, and barrage of living expenses, he really didn't have as much money saved up as one would've thought he did.

In total, Great had about $200,000 saved up. He owed Flaco $150,000 and he had the $200,000 neatly stacked in the duffel bags already prepared for him. He was waiting on $100,000 from Luke and Rello to get him there.

Great was now faced with a decision. Should he pay Flaco out of his safe and start all over again? Or should he say, *Fuck Flaco* and find him another connect?

As he weighed his options, he thought about how nobody else would be able to match the $15,000 price that Flaco was charging him per brick. Everybody else was either taxing or nervous to deal with him because he stayed on so much bullshit.

Great was what most connects considered a high risk. He continuously brought undo heat upon himself from doing things that he didn't need to do. Flaco was the only one, willing to take the risks of dealing with him.

After realizing that two and two equaled four, no matter if you add it or multiply it, Great quickly decided that he'd just have to start over. With a connect like Flaco, it wouldn't take long for him to get back, so he figured…

CHAPTER NINE

It was a bright and sunny day. Everybody in the hood was outside. The parks were packed with kids running around and the teenagers were gathered in their own little packs roaming the hood. The smell of freshly mown lawns filled the air as homeowners took advantage of the beautiful weather and spruced up their yards.

Jilla kept dialing Destiny's number to tell her to come outside but her phone continuously went directly to the voicemail. Luckily, he had Dusty with him, so he sent him to knock on the door and ask for her. Jilla wasn't into the meeting the parent's thing so by Destiny and Dusty being cousins, he was the perfect person to get her outside.

Jilla had bought himself an '87 candy coated, midnight blue, Oldsmobile *Cutlass* with silver flakes in the paint. It was sitting on Vogue tires and two-bladed Bose rims. The Alpine sound system he had inside it could be heard from blocks away when he had it cranked up. This was the perfect day for him to show off his new whip and his new girl, both at the same time.

Destiny and Jilla had been talking on and off over the

phone. Today she finally agreed to let him pick her up if he'd take her to the carnival that had arrived at 95th and the Dan Ryan. Jilla made sure he'd just come from getting his car detailed so it would be shining like it had just came off the show room floor.

When Destiny came out of the house, she still remained as beautiful and flawless as Jilla had remembered her to be from the night of his party. She was wearing an all-white Puma tennis skirt, a pink and white Puma shirt, and some pink and white Puma gym shoes. Her hair was done in a wrap style that came down to her shoulders and her ears were adorned with a pair of gold hoop earrings. They accentuated the small herringbone necklace, with the *D* charm, that she wore around her neck. Jilla couldn't understand, for the world, how he'd gone so long without spotting her.

"And your name is?" A voice out of nowhere spoke, breaking Jilla out of the trance that Destiny's beauty had him entrapped in.

He was so caught up in admiration that he hadn't seen the lady come out of the house after Destiny.

"Huh? Oh! My name is Jilla." he replied nervously, figuring the lady to be Destiny's mother.

"I know your mother didn't name you no Jilla did she?" Destiny's mom asked, inspecting him from head to toe.

"No ma'am, my name is Justin." Jilla stuttered, "Justin Carter." he lied hoping the fake name would be enough to satisfy her curiosity.

"Okay, Justin Carter." she said turning her nose up at him "Make sure you have my daughter in by 7:00 p.m. because she has to get ready for school tomorrow. I got the license plate number off them temporary things u got on the back of this car, so if you're not here by seven I'm calling the police." she said with one hand on her hip and the other holding a pad and a pencil.

"This is a pretty decked out car for someone your age to be driving too. And where you get all that jewelry you got on from?" she asked.

"Maaa!" Destiny cut in as she was getting inside the car and shutting the door.

Dusty was in the back seat giggling from seeing Jilla sweat and Destiny suffering from embarrassment.

"Okay, I'mma let y'all go ahead on. You better not let nothing happen to my baby." Destiny's mother finally said.

"Yes ma'am." Jilla replied, glad Destiny had gotten him off the hook from having to suffer any more interrogation.

Jilla started up his car and pulled off. As he turned the corner, he cranked up the music and let Jay-Z beat out of his speakers.

Destiny couldn't help but notice how crisp Jilla was dressed himself. She liked his swag. That was one of the main reasons she gave him some rhythm in the first place. Most of the other boys in their age group were dirty. Not Jilla though, never.

Just like she was matching from head to toe, so was he. He had on a pair of freshly pressed Coogi shorts, a white and baby blue North Carolina Tarheels T-shirt, some baby blue and white Air Jordan's, and a blue North Carolina fitted cap. Around his neck, hung a chain that came down to his stomach. Dangling from it was a money sign charm. His right earring was a letter *J* and his left earring was a letter *G*. Damn she liked his style.

Pulling up to the projects, Jilla threw the car in park to let Lil Dusty out. He popped the trunk from inside the glove box so Dusty could get the bag of clothes out. He'd bought tailor made suits from Mr. Kays for them to wear to the funeral.

"Bye Tony." Destiny said, calling Dusty by his government name.

"Aight y'all." he replied, heading towards the hallway of the building.

"Tell Colors I'll be back later on." Jilla said, as he put his foot on the brake and threw the car in drive. "And if Great calls, or comes through, tell him I'll be back in time for us to get to the restaurant tonight.

Great had told Jilla that they were going to holler at Flaco. Every time he went to see him, Great would always take Jilla along. There wasn't one aspect of the game that Great didn't make it his business to try and show Jilla. Plus, Flaco had taken a liking to the young nigga Jilla himself ever since he heard about how he'd gotten down on Speedy and Geno.

As Jilla was about to pull off, Camelle came walking around the corner. Her, Tanya, and Cheri were on their way to the candy store. When she peeped Destiny in the passenger seat of Jilla's new whip she became infuriated.

"This nigga got the nerve to have this bitch in the passenger seat of the car that I helped him buy!" she said to Cheri and Tanya, making sure they were seeing the same thing she was.

Camelle wasn't only upset, her heart was shattered as well. After all she'd done for Jilla, nothing seemed to be enough to stop him from messing around with other girls.

Jilla caught eye contact with Camelle after looking up from adjusting the volume on the CD player. Knowing that she'd peeped Destiny in the car with him, he quickly pulled off before Camelle got the chance to come up to the car and make a scene. He knew what Camelle was capable of doing and he didn't want her to run Destiny off before he got a chance to put her under his spell.

* * * *

At the carnival, Destiny and Jilla walked and talked, getting to know each other a little bit. While they were in the car, they never spoke a word to one another. They just rode in silence, vibing to the music. The carnival atmosphere loosened them up though. They rode on rides, Jilla won Destiny teddy bears, and he bought her everything she asked for from the concession stands.

Camelle kept blowing Jilla's cell phone up and leaving him nasty messages throughout the entire time that he and Destiny were at the carnival. Jilla had to put his phone on vibrate in hopes that Destiny wouldn't become as irritated as he was from Camelle's consistency. This was the first time that him and Destiny got to kick it together and he had no plans on letting Camelle ruin the moment.

"I want us to take a picture together." Destiny whined in a baby's voice' as they walked up on a picture booth.

Even if he wanted to deny her request, Jilla couldn't. It was something about that voice that made him melt like butter.

Jilla paid the photographer for a picture. As the flash from the camera went off, Jilla's cell phone was steadily vibrating. He couldn't turn it off just in case Great tried to call him. As they hugged for the picture, Destiny felt it vibrating against her stomach. She knew it was Camelle blowing him up because he didn't answer it. Plus, even though Jilla didn't know, she peeped Camelle and her friends looking at them as they pulled off from the projects. She knew the two of them were an item, but Destiny was confident that if she applied herself, she would eventually win Jilla over. She wanted Jilla, and she was willing to be patient to get what she wanted.

"I can put you-all's picture in a frame, on a button, on a balloon, or on a t-shirt. Which one will it be?" asked the picture man.

"On a button." answered Destiny. "That way I can attach it to my heart if I ever feel the need."

The photographer put the picture on a button and handed it to Jilla. Before Jilla handed it to Destiny, he looked at it, impressed with how good she and him looked together.

"Our first date." Destiny said as she looked at the picture.

The word date stood out to Jilla. He had never taken a girl out on an actual date before. Usually he would just ride around with girls, smokin' weed and getting them drunk. Then he would take them somewhere to try and get inside their pants. Destiny had called for something different because she didn't smoke or drink. This made her all the more interesting to him.

"Yeah, our first date." Jilla responded while taking his cell phone out of his pocket to check the time. "Speaking of firsts, it's about time for me to get you home before your moms make 9 the first of three numbers she dial on her phone."

Exchanging laughs, they both made their way back to Jilla's car. Jilla had enjoyed himself on his and Destiny's first date. It was something he could see himself getting used to.

After they pulled back up in front of Destiny's house, Jilla walked her to the door carrying the four teddy bears that he had won for her. He gave her a goodbye hug and made sure she got into the house safe.

CHAPTER TEN

Great and Jilla rode north on the Dan Ryan expressway. They were headed to meet Flaco at the restaurant. Every time he viewed the scenery of the downtown Chicago area, Jilla loved it. To him, it was like escaping from the hood. Great had introduced him to a lot of new things since he'd taken him up under his wing. Jilla was learning the game fast. He was destined to be a thorough leader.

As they navigated through the streets of downtown, Jilla always seemed to feel the ultimate rush of excitement. Especially as they cruised down Michigan Avenue. Even though the stores were closed, and the streets weren't packed with their usual array of, "upper-class shoppers", just the sight of the elite names of fashion plastered on the store fronts kept him in a state of awe. He'd only heard of those high-end fashion names in rap songs. Gucci, Prada, Polo, Burberry, Fendi, Salvatore Ferragamo, etc. You name it and they all were posted up and down Michigan Avenue.

The Magnificent Mile is what the strip was better known as. Based on the large sums of money spent up and down the block every day, the name suited it well. Every time Jilla took that ride with Great passed the Magnificent Mile for any reason, it always served as a constant reminder and motivating force for him to step his game up.

The vibration of his cell phone interrupted Jilla from his deep thought. He looked at the caller ID and saw that it was Camelle. Knowing that he was going to have to listen to her bullshit eventually, he figured he'd might as well go ahead and get it over with.

Just as he was about to accept the call, his phone stopped ringing. Jilla had taken so long contemplating whether to answer it or not, he had missed the call.

"Who you duckin' lil nigga?" Great asked with an inquisitive look on his face. "Don't tell me you got stalkers now like the G.R.E.A.T." he continued, now sporting across his face the proud look of a father whose son had just mimicked an act of his very own.

"Hell yeah, that bitch Camelle caught me wit' my new dip and she been blowing me up ever since." Jilla replied while looking at his cell phone aggravatingly.

As soon as Jilla finished his sentence his phone rang again. This time, he answered it on the first ring. "Whassup?"

"Bitch ass nigga, don't *whassup* me. You know what the fuck is up." Camelle loved to use the *B* word, even though she knew it guaranteed her an ass whooping every time she did it, she still didn't give a fuck. "You must've dropped your lil hoe off ore something cuz now you can answer the mufuckin phone. Nigga you ain't shit! I'm sittin' up here stealing from my own cousin, tryin to help yo' ass, and you got the nerve to have some other bitch riding around in the new car that I helped you buy?!! Then you act like you can't even answer—" Jilla held the phone away from his ear and let Camelle talk to herself until he no longer heard her hollering. He then put it back up to his ear.

"Man, I ain't trying to hear that shit. You been acting shady as hell lately. You don't love me. I asked you to let me get dat nigga Shotgun, but you act like you love him instead of me or some shit." Jilla snapped, forgetting that he was riding in the car with Great.

He didn't want Great to know about how he was scheming on sticking up Shotgun because he knew Great would try and trick him into telling him about the lick. Or, he would try to manipulate Jilla in to giving him the money when he had finally gotten it. Especially after he'd just taken such a loss with Luke and Rello's deaths.

"Nigga quit playing. You know damn well that the only reason I won't let you do that shit is because of my cousin. Fuck you anyway though. Tell that bitch Destiny to let you stick up somebody." Camelle shot back.

Great was pulling up to the street that Flaco's restaurant was located on. Not only were the wheels in his head spinning about how he was going to approach Flaco, but he was also thinking about how he was going to squeeze Jilla for some more info about what he'd overheard him saying about

Shotgun.

"Yeah whatever. I ain't trying to hear all this bullshit you talkin' about. I got to get ready to go and take care of something right fast. When you get ready to make me know that you love me, then you can hit me back. Until then, I'm outta here."

Jilla hung up his cell phone before Camelle could get another word in. As they pulled into the parking lot behind the restaurant, he powered it off. He knew Camelle was going to keep blowing his phone up and he didn't want it interrupting Great and Flaco while they were conducting business. As he powered off the phone, he was silently thinking about Camelle. Hoping his little plan was working.

* * * *

La Exquisita was a well-known Latin restaurant tucked away in the northern corner of downtown Chicago. Great and Jilla entered through the rear door, which lead right to Flaco's office. Julian, Flaco's bodyguard, ushered them in. They were then instructed, by a motion of a finger from Flaco, to have a seat on the Italian leather sofa that sat inside the plushly decorated office.

Flaco sat at his desk, with his feet propped up on it, engaged in a telephone conversation. Between every few words he took a puff off of the Cuban Cigar he held in his hand. Flaco held his telephone conversation in Spanish so that Great and Jilla couldn't understand just what it was that he was discussing. By the tone of his voice, and the ear to ear smile that he was sporting, it appeared to be good news that he was getting. Great hoped that this would make the chances of his proposition more favorable.

"Sorry for the wait my friends. Flaco said to Great and Jilla in his thick Spanish accent."

He interrupted them from their fixation on watching the beautiful women of *'Caliente'*. Three 52" plasma screen televisions were posted up around his office. Women in bikinis were running around scantily dressed on each one of them.

Flaco stood up, walked around his desk, and extended his hand to Great and Jilla. One by one, he shook their hands.

"I've just learned that I've been blessed with a new grandson. What'll you guys be drinking?" Flaco said as he made his way to the mini bar that sat directly across the room from his desk.

Great was happy for him but decided to decline the drink and cut the small talk. He needed a clear mindstate so that he could be persuasive as possible if he needed to.

"I'm cool Flaco. Congratulations though, and thanks for the offer." Great replied.

"Yeah, congratulations Flaco. You know I don't drink but I will take a bottled water if you got one." Jilla responded.

Flaco fixed himself a drink and grabbed Jilla a bottled water. He then focused on Great who looked as if something was bothering him.

"It seems as if you have some things weighing heavily on your mind my friend. You're not your usual spunky self." Flaco opened.

"Nah man, it's just that shits been real fucked up for me the last couple of days Flac. You know I just lost my two niggaz and shit. Plus $100,000 on top of that. I mean, I got all the money I owe you in them duffel bags there." Great explained while motioning to the two bags of money he had sat on the floor next to the couch he and Jilla were sitting on. "But the money I usually give you up front, for my half of the deal, I ain't got. And I gotta pay for my two niggaz funerals at that. I know all of this might sound personal and shit, but I need you to look out for me on the front side this trip. You know I ain't never came short with your bread and I always keep shit neat with you. I need you this rip though."

Jilla couldn't believe his ears. He thought Great was rich. Never in a million years could someone have convinced him that Great could even be close to hurting. This was the day that he learned that everything that glittered wasn't gold.

Flaco sat in thought for about 30 seconds. The room was so silent that you could've heard an ant pissing on cotton. He knew Great was a risky gamble the moment he agreed to fronting him whatever he bought. Now Great was asking him to completely front him everything, 20 kilos. Flaco knew Great was a certified cocaine dealer and Great had never been anything less than loyal to him. He had made a lot of money for him since they'd began doing business and by the look in his eyes, he could tell that Great was as thirsty as a Mountain Lion. But a 20-kilo front sure was asking for a lot.

"I tell you what Great." Flaco said, while looking at him sternly. "I know you've really taken a rough hit. The only way to truly be successful in this business that we're in, is to have good money management skills. For you to lose out on

$100,000 and claim to be broke, that is unacceptable coming from a member of my team. Jilla, I want you to learn from this as well. You cannot spend your money beyond your means. In this game it's not how much you make, but how much you put up that counts. With that said, no, I will not front you the 20 kilos."

Greats heart sunk into his chest when he heard those words leave out of Flaco's mouth. Jilla couldn't believe his ears either. He was wondering how he could get down on Great like that knowing how much work he'd been moving for him.

"But!" Flaco said interrupting Great and Jilla's thoughts.

"What I will do is I'll front you 15 of them."

Great's hurt and disappointment turned into bliss and relief. He thought Flaco had left him hanging and crossed him, but he didn't. He came through for him and the 15 bricks were more than enough for him to get back on his feet with. He learned a couple of lessons from all of this. The most important one being to stack his bread and never allow himself to be put in this situation again. So, he thought...

Great got the 15 bricks from Flaco, then he and Jilla went on their way. Great was now on a mission. He had to bounce back like never before. Great dropped Jilla off at the spot, sending him upstairs with one of the bricks, and headed home. After the funeral he planned on trapping like never before.

CHAPTER ELEVEN

Luke and Rello's funeral was more like a fashion show/ get-together. They had a double funeral with hustlers and chicks from all over the city in attendance. Jeffery Manor, Lawn City, Pocket Town, Lakeside, Princeton Park, Englewood, Dark Side, The Low—end, The West Side, The Wild-Hundreds, and The North Pole, were just some of the sets that came to pay homage.

Bury me a G by Tupac; *R.I.P.* by Spice 1; *Gangsta Lean*, by D.R.S.; and *I miss my homies* by Master P; were just a few of the songs that spilled into the ears of the mourners. Great, Luke, and Rello always demanded that their departures from God's green earth be in that fashion.

Man, when I go play rap songs at my funeral. Fuck all that sad shit. They would all say to one another as they kicked it until the wee hours of a many mornings. That's exactly how Great buried his guys too. To rap music, and both decked out in their tailor-made Prada suits.

After the funeral, everyone headed out to the Joe River Center for the repast. This was located in the south suburbs of Harvey, Illinois. It was more like an afterparty, but Great knew that this was exactly what his guys would've wanted. People shot craps, drank, danced, and partied. It was something like a celebration of Luke and Rello's relief from life's everyday struggles of living by the code of the streets.

Great just sat back in the corner of his table with Lynn, downing shot after shot of Cognac, and puffing on blunt after blunt. His guys were gone and all he wanted to do was numb the pain that he was feeling. All that was on his mind was getting his money right and, twenty-one gun saluting anybody who even acted like they wanted it.

* * * *

"You straight fool?" Jilla asked Great as he stumbled to his car, leaning on Lynn's shoulder, with his .40 caliber out and in his hand.

Great was plastered and Jilla knew it. Luckily, Lynn was with him, and she hadn't been drinking so she could get him home safely.

"Yeah I'm straight my lil dude." Great slurred as Lynn opened the passenger side of her BMW truck to place Great inside. "Especially when I got both my bitches with me." Great assured him, referring to Lynn and his .40 Cal., which he was now holding in the air so that Jilla could see it.

"Aight *G,* I'll holla at you tomorrow." Jilla said as him, Colors, and Dusty headed towards his car.

Lynn jumped inside of her driver's seat, put on her seat belt, and began going through her C.D. case looking for some Mary J. Blige to listen to. Settling on her *Share My World* C.D., she slid it in the C.D. changer. Just as she placed it in, and was about to pull off, Jilla came running up to the truck and tapped on the window. *Tap! Tap! Tap!*

Lynn jumped. "Boy you scared the shit out of me!" She hollered, holding her hand over her heart while using her free one to press the button, letting her window down.

"My bad, I forgot to give this to Great." Jilla replied while handing her a Jewels-Osco grocery bag filled with money. "Tell him we probably got enough to last until tomorrow afternoon but that's it. So he gone have to come holla at us as soon as he get up." Jilla instructed her, seeing that Great was in the passenger seat passed out.

"Aight boy." Lynn replied with one hand still on her heart, tossing the bag on the back seat with the other. "Y'all drive safe and don't get pulled over with all them damn guns in the car either." she said as she began to pull off.

Jilla headed to his car, not knowing that it would be the last time he saw Great, or Lynn, alive and breathing.

* * * *

Beep beep... Beep beep... "Spot 'em got 'em!" Money spoke through the chirper of his Nextel, letting them know that Great and Lynn were about to pull up to the underground parking garage of their building.

"Yep, Yep." Mo replied through the chirper, as he flicked

the remainder of his Newport cigarette out the window of the all black, tinted out Chevy Impala.

"It's showtime baby boy." Y.B. said, checking his Glock 9, making sure it was a bullet in the chamber. "Time to cook the doughnuts."

* * * *

Wednesday, you went away. Thursday, things weren't the same, Lynn sang along as Mary J's, *Seven Days* crooned out of her factory installed Bose speakers. As she pulled into the underground parking garage of their building, she looked over at Great hoping that she wouldn't have her hands full getting him on the elevator and upstairs.

She backed into parking spot #6, the one that cost Great an extra $200 a month and was reserved specifically for her vehicle. "Baby get up, we're home." Lynn said, as she pulled the keys out of the ignition.

She reached in the back seat, grabbed the bag of money that Jilla had given her, and shook Great in another attempt to wake him up.

"What? Whassup? Where we at?" Great asked, waking up and grabbing his gun out of his lap.

"Baby calm down, we at home." Lynn said, as she stepped out of the driver's seat.

Great looked around noticing the familiar setting of the garage, opened the door, and stepped out of the passenger seat of the truck. Still drunk, he tucked the .40 Cal in the waistline of his navy-blue dress pants. Lynn activated the alarm from her key chain, and then her and Great headed to the elevator hand in hand.

Click, Click! Great heard close to his ear as he felt the cold steel pressed against his temple. "One false move boy and on my momma, I'mma blow your motherfuckin brains out." Mo spat as he held the Desert Eagle firmly against Great's head.

"Baby girl, no noise please." Y.B. said to Lynn, seeing that she was so terrified she looked like she was about to scream. "You too pretty for me to have to splatter your head all over the door of this here elevator." Y.B. continued, as he relieved her of the grocery bag with the money in it.

Great instantly sobered up, he was heated. He couldn't believe he had let these cats get the ups on him. The last time he was in this predicament, Jilla saved his life. This time he was all by his lonely.

"You know what it is. Tuffy ain't so tuff now is he?" Mo said while holding Great at gunpoint with one hand and patting him down with the other. He pulled Great's .40 Cal from the waist of his slacks and placed it in the small of his back. He then made sure Great didn't have any more heat on him before pushing him towards the stairwell.

"Make your next move your best move and head toward those stairs." Mo directed Great. He decided that it would be better to take the stairwell because it would be less of a chance of running into neighbors and there weren't any cameras.

The four of them hiked up the stairs. Great and Lynn in front leading, Mo and Y.B. following with their guns pressed against the backs of Great and Lynn's heads. When they

reached the floor that they lived on, they went to the door and
Y.B. instructed Lynn to unlock it. She complied, and they all
entered the penthouse.

Mo locked the door and Y.B. threw Great and Lynn onto
the living room couch. Reaching inside the front pocket of his
black hoodie, Y.B. pulled out a roll of Duct tape. They taped
both Lynn and Great by the wrists and ankles. Then it was time
for the get down.

"Aight gangsta-ass Great." Y.B. said flashing a sly smile.
"This is the part where you lead me to the money, and I take
every single red cent you got up in this mufucka.

Lynn was crying hysterically, leaving mascara lines
running down her face.

"I ain't leading you two pussy mufuckas nowhere. Fuck
y'all. Y'all might as well kill me." Great replied.

Lynn looked over at him like he was crazy.

The flashbacks of how Great, Luke, Rello, and Jilla had
done him began to replay inside of Y.B.'s mind. Before he
knew it, he fired shot, after shot, after shot, into Great's body
until he left him lifeless.

Lynn was so petrified that she urinated and defecated on
herself. Mo immediately began to go and search the crib
because he knew some nosey neighbor probably heard the
gunshots and most likely called the police. They had to hurry
up and get up out of there.

"Okay, bitch! It's your turn." Y.B. declared to Lynn, aiming
his gun at her face with nothing but murder in his eyes. "Where
the mufu— Before he could finish his question, Mo ran back
into the living room interrupting him. "I found the safe in the

bedroom. It ain't open though.

Y.B. pointed his gun at Lynn's heart. She knew he wasn't playing any games due to how he had just done Great. "Bitch I know you know the combination." he spat, ready to blow her heart out of her chest.

Lynn looked over at Great, filled with more holes than a Wiffle Ball, and immediately got to spitting out numbers like a lottery machine. "11-17-05." she said, hoping that she had just saved her own life. Little did she know, her chances for survival were none.

Mo ran back into the bedroom and punched the combination into the safe. The door popped open and jackpot, it was filled with bricks. Seeing that he didn't have anything to put them in, he ran over to the bed and snatched the pillowcases off two pillows. He ran back to the safe and loaded the bricks into them. He then searched the room a little more, looking for some more cash, but came up empty.

"We good my nigga." Mo said to Y.B., tossing him one of the cases.

He was happier than a kid on Christmas. "Let's get up outta here fool. You know them people probably on the way." Mo said while Y.B. examined the contents of the pillowcase.

"Ain't no more cash?" Y.B. asked, figuring that they wouldn't have come up with more cash than what they had in the Jewels-Osco bag.

"Ain't none in there." Mo replied.

"Damn! We straight with this though." Headed towards the door, Y.B. then looked over at Lynn. "Handle her." he instructed.

Just like they were splitting the money, they had to split the murders as well. He wasn't leaving no room for a cross out.

"Sorry sweetheart, I wish I could let your fine ass live, but you know how it goes. No witnesses, no case. And I'm too sexy for jail."

With that said, Mo placed a bullet right between Lynn's eyes along with three more inside her chest.

They ran down the stairs and to their car. As they pulled off, Y.B. grabbed the blunt off the ashtray, lit it up, and said, "I love it when a plan comes together."

CHAPTER TWELVE

Riding around the East-Side in his Cutlass, with a 10 Millimeter in his lap, Jilla listened to Tupac's, *Pain*. He had just got through dropping Camelle off at her grandmother's house and now he was just bending blocks, thinking about everything that was going on.

Within a months' time, Great, Luke, and Rello had died. The little money that they had left at the spot was given to Great's mom for his funeral and Camelle was still acting funny about letting him stick up Shotgun.

Dusty and Colors didn't know how to save their money. They just spent everything on clothes, weed, and other miscellaneous things. Jilla spent his money on these things as well but he always put something in the stash.

I need to call a roundtable meeting, Jilla thought to himself as he pulled up to White Castles on 95th and Jeffery. While he was waiting in the drive-thru for his order, he hit Colors and Dusty on their cell phones and told them to meet him at the spot. He knew it was time for him to step up, so he had to put a plan into effect.

* * * *

Jilla pulled up to the projects. When he got upstairs to the spot, Colors and Dusty were playing the video game, waiting on him to arrive. Red was there as well. She had Strawberry and Passion with her. They were girls, but they were part of the family as well and needed to be in attendance.

"Look," Jilla said as he powered off the television so he could get everyone's undivided attention. "I know shit is all fucked up now wit Great and them being gone. But I know for a fact that they wouldn't want us moping around, or falling off, like we some type of weaklings or some shit." He then dug inside of his shorts pocket, pulled out two rolls of money with rubber bands around them, and threw them on the cocktail table in front of everybody.

"This all I got to my name." he said, patting his pockets and opening his arms as if to say what's up. "It's thirty-two hundred dollars. I'mma buy some work and *Break Bread* with everybody. We family and we gone come up together. The show ain't stopping though. The only problem is we need a connect until we can save up enough money so I can go holler at Great's old connect."

"I can holla at my cousin over there in Terror-Town. Him and his guys be doing they thang. And he been tryin' to get me to fuck with him too." Colors pitched in.

Colors' cousin and his guys had been supplying the East-Side ever since Great had gotten killed.

"Bet, we on then." Jilla said, rubbing the palms of his hands together. "From this day on, we *Bar None*. And any mufucka that cross the family —

"Say no more," Dusty said, interrupting Jilla and picking up the .32 automatic off of the table.

"Aight then. Everybody put they hand in this circle and on three we say, *Bar None*!"

"*BAR NONE*!!!" They all shouted in unison. That was the day the *Bar None* bond officially became established.

CHAPTER THIRTEEN

Jilla was sitting in front of Destiny's house, waiting for her to come to the car. He couldn't wait to see her pretty face. When she stepped out of the door in a pair of white Capri pants, brown sandals, and a brown and gold fitted T-shirt, Jilla couldn't help but think to himself, *Damn, this the baddest lil bitch I've ever seen in real life.*

Jilla wasn't used to seeing the type of innocent beauty that Destiny possessed. He only saw that on television. Not only was she beautiful, but Destiny dressed with class and was deep off into her schoolbooks. Destiny was like a step above the types of girls he was used to dealing with. She was more mature.

As Destiny entered the car, Jilla was instantly greeted with the intoxicating scent of the perfume she wore. He didn't know the name of it, but whatever it was, it turned him on. Her nails were French manicured, and her lips were perfectly coated with lip gloss that accentuated her caramel skin tone. Her presence just made him feel different. A good type of different.

"Hey." Destiny greeted as she pulled the passenger door

shut. All 32 of her perfect pearly whites were showing and she was looking him directly in the eyes.

"What up with you? Looking all beautiful I see." Jilla rebutted, not aware that the words he uttered were being dictated by the trance her light brown eyes had him in.

"Thank you." she said, giving Jilla the once over and liking what she saw as well. Jilla was sporting' a plain blue T-shirt, some Jordan blue jeans, and some blue and white Jordan 3's. His hair was freshly cut against the grain, with the sides and back tapered. Everything about him looked brand new.

While at Bennigan's, Jilla and Destiny sat across the table from one another discussing the latest music, videos, fashion, and neighborhood gossip. Even though Destiny didn't hang out in the streets much, she surprisingly was in the know of the things happening in the hood.

After they left the restaurant, they caught the 5:05 p.m. show and went to watch, *Big Mama's House.* They shared a medium sized popcorn along with several other items from the concession area. Destiny sat on Jilla's lap throughout the entire movie and felt as though she was slowly but surely carving her name into his heart.

Once back inside the car, after the movie, Jilla pulled his 10 Millimeter from under his seat and placed it on his lap. He then powered his cell phone back on. He had 13 voice mail messages. Destiny checked her phone and she had voice mail messages as well.

* * * *

During the drive home, Destiny was on her cell filling

79

Michelle in on the movie that her and Jilla had just watched. While she was doing that, Jilla was busying himself checking his messages.

Eight of them were from fiends alerting him that he was missing money, two were from Colors and Dusty trying to figure out where he was, and three were from Camelle telling him that he needed to call her A.S.A.P. He figured Camelle either heard about him being with Destiny or she had another blessing for him out of Shotgun's stash. Whichever of the two it was, he was soon about to find out.

Jilla pulled up and double parked in front of Destiny's house and they exchanged their goodbyes. "I had fun with you today." Jilla told her.

Destiny held her head down, chewing on some gum, trying to figure out how to break the news to him that she had. "Damn, you look like I made you sad instead of glad?" Jilla quipped.

"No, it's not that. I've been trying to figure out the right moment to tell you this."

"Tell me what?"

"Jilla, I'm leaving to go to college. But I really like you and I don't want to leave you."

"Well why you leaving?"

"Cause I can't be around here like these other bitches you're used to messing around with." Destiny said while waving her hand in a 180-degree circle like she was gesturing towards an audience. "I have to graduate from college and be something in life."

Jilla just sat there nonchalantly, taking in everything Destiny was saying. "I feel you on that. It's all good. We can still talk on the phone, and you get to come home on holidays, right?"

"Yeah."

"And I can come where you at too, right?"

"Yeah. But the question is are you going to stay in contact with me?"

"Hell yeah I am. I'm feelin' you shorty. I like your style. Ever since I first saw you you've been on my mind."

"Yeah right. I bet you tell all the girls that."

"All what girls?" Jilla rebutted, trying to display a sense of innocence.

"You know what girls I'm talking about. You just need to know that I like you for you, not what you got."

Jilla was at a loss for words. Destiny had caught him off guard with that one.

Destiny checked the rear-view mirror on the passenger side door to make sure no cars were coming before she opened it. After she stepped one foot outside, she said, "I'll talk to you later." and gave him a kiss on the cheek.

Jilla just stared at her blankly as she walked off. He couldn't help but think to himself, *Damn, I'm gone miss her fine ass.*

Once she entered the house, Jilla threw the cutty in drive and pulled off. He was missing too much money and he had to get back on the grind.

* * * *

Before Jilla even made it off the corner of Destiny's block, he dialed up Colors cell phone and let him know that he was right around the corner. He then called up the fiends and let them know that they could meet him at the spot if they still wanted to cop some work. By the time he'd gotten through calling them all up, he'd made it to the projects.

Jilla pulled into the parking lot and parked his car so that it could be seen out of the kitchen window of the spot. He tucked his pistol in his waistline, looked around to make sure there weren't any police in sight, hopped out of the car, and closed the door behind him.

As he made his way to the hallway of the building his cell phone rang.

Looking at the caller ID, and noticing a South suburban area code, from Chicago Heights, he became curious as to who it could've been and answered it.

"Hello." Jilla answered, while making his way up the hallway stairs two steps at a time.

"Where you at? the voice on the other end of the phone inquired.

"At the spot." Jilla informed.

He had now caught on to the all familiar voice on the other end. It was Camelle. "How come you ain't been answering your phone?" she began. Jilla entered the spot and threw up the *Bar None* sign to Red.

Locking the door, he walked into the living room where Colors and Dusty were engaged in a crap game. "You musta been in the spot wit' one of your hoes."

"Yeah aight." Jilla said. "I was shootin' dice so I ain't hear my phone ringing." he lied. "Anyway, what's up? Where you at?" he asked, redirecting the 21 questions towards her.

"I'm over my cousin's house." she responded.

"Yeah, so what you on?" Jilla asked her.

"Lookin' at two grocery bags full of money." she

responded.

Jilla's eyes widened as if he'd just seen a ghost. He tapped Dusty on the shoulder and held up his index finger motioning for him and Colors to hold up a second so he could make sure he'd heard what he thought he did.

"What you say?" he asked Camelle in search of reassurance.

"I said, I'm looking at two grocery bags full of money." she reassured him.

Colors and Dusty were looking at Jilla frantically, trying to figure out who he was on the phone with. More importantly, they wondered what they were talking about and what was so important that their dice game had to be delayed. Especially Colors, he was down and was trying to win his money back from Dusty.

"How much is it?" Jilla asked Camelle, looking back and forth between Dusty and Colors, motioning for Dusty to pass him the blunt he'd just fired up.

"I don't know, but it's two big grocery bags full." Camelle replied causing Jilla to start choking on the weed smoke he'd just inhaled.

In between chokes he replied, "You gone...let...me come through...there and get that shit?"

"Yeah, but you know what you gone have to do." Camelle informed him. She had finally gave in and took care of that business.

"Aight bet." Jilla agreed. "Just give me the directions and I'm on my way."

Camelle gave the directions to Jilla and he flipped his cell phone close. He then let Colors, Dusty, and Red in on the conversation that had just taken place.

It seemed like Jilla had been waiting forever for this day to come and it had finally arrived. However, he had one hell of a question on his mind. How much was in them bags???

* * * *

The lick went down smooth. Jilla and Colors pulled up in front of the address that Camelle had given them. He called her cell phone and let her know that he was outside. After she came to the front door, they hopped out of the car and went in.

"Where your cousin at?" Jilla asked, making a visual scan of the perimeter from where he was standing in the living room. Dusty and Colors were standing right behind him, guns in hand.

"She gone to the club with her friends." Camelle responded, shutting and locking the front door.

The living room was decked out with black leather furniture, a fancy TV., wall to wall mirrors, and expensive looking lamps. It looked like it had money in it.

"Where shorty at?" Jilla asked, referring to the baby.

Usually Trevon would be running around, causing havoc, but Jilla hadn't seen him. "He in the room sleep." replied Camelle.

Her saying that relieved Jilla of his worry about Trevon seeing his face. Trevon had been in the projects, a many of times, with Camelle and would be able to recognize him when he'd seen him. Even though he was only two years old He still spoke well enough to pronounce Jilla's name. Then it was time for the ultimate question. "Where the money at?"

Camelle smiled sheepishly and led them to the bedroom.

She turned the light switch on and walked over to the closet, opening the door.

Jilla, Colors, and Dusty couldn't believe their eyes. Sitting in front of their faces were two brown grocery bags filled with money. All three of their mouths immediately dropped. Jilla began grabbing one of the bags and Colors followed suit, grabbing the other one.

"Unh, unh." Camelle said, grabbing Jilla's hand, stopping him from picking up the bag of money. "You know what you gotta do first." *This lil hot ass bitch*, Jilla thought to himself as he released the grip on the bag.

He then told Dusty and Colors to toss the house up, take the bags to the car, and wait for him out there. He told them to make it look like someone had actually come through and pulled off a stick up. While they ransacked the house, Jilla took Camelle in another one of the bedrooms and gave her what she wanted.

After Jilla and Camelle got done sexin' they both came out of the bedroom. While Camelle came out giddily, Jilla was back on business. He went into each room of the house and made sure Colors and Dusty had done an adequate job of tossing up the place. Satisfied that it did indeed look as if an armed robbery took place, he then went over the story that Camelle was supposed to tell her cousin.

"Tell her that somebody knocked on the door and you opened it to see who it was. When you opened the door, it was three dudes with ski-masks on and they pointed guns in your face and pushed you inside the crib. One of the dudes made you sit on the couch with his gun pointed at you, while the other two dudes searched the house. They then came out the room with two bags of money and left."

"Okay." Camelle replied. "I got it."

"Make sure when you call her that you act like you cryin' and shit scared as hell." he continued to coach her.

"Okaaayyy!" Camelle agreed again.

"Aight, we boutta get up outta here before somebody fuck around and pop up on us while we here. When you get back home make sure you call and let me know how everything went down."

Jilla then left out the house and trotted down the walkway to the car. After he jumped in, him, Dusty, and Colors headed to the expressway. On the ride back to the spot, all of them had the same thing on their minds. *How much money was in them bags?*

Once inside the spot, Jilla, Red, Colors, and Dusty all counted the money together. The total turned out to be $399, 750.00. Jilla couldn't believe his eyes. This was what he'd been itching for, his time to shine. And it was now here.

CHAPTER FOURTEEN

Jilla had never possessed so much money in his life. He gave Dusty, Colors, and Red $50,000 each. He then put the rest of the money back into two bags and dialed Destiny's cell phone number.

"Hello." Destiny answered sounding like she'd just been awaken out of her sleep.

"Wake up sleepy head." Jilla said, smiling, wondering if she looked as beautiful as usual as soon as she woke up.

"Boy! What you doing calling me this late?" Destiny asked him as she gazed up at the alarm clock that sat next to her bed. "It's three-thirty in the morning Jilla. Are you crazy?"

"Naw, I'm sorry. Something came up and I need you to do a favor for me. I'm on my way over there."

"You can't come over here this late. My momma will have a fit."

"Yeah, I know. I'mma just come to your room window and give you something. You the only person I can trust. I'mma text you as soon as I pull up."

"I'm the only on you can trust? Trust with what?"

"It ain't shit but some money. Stop panicking."

"Alright Jilla. You better hurry up. You know I gotta go to school in the morning. You better be quiet too so you don't wake my momma up."

"Okay, I'm on my way right now."

After dropping one of the bags of money off at Destiny's house, Jilla then went and dropped the other one off at his mother's house. After he was done, he returned to the spot and fell asleep on the couch.

The next morning Jilla, Colors, Dusty and Red all got up and headed car shopping. Dust bought a Chevy Impala, Colors bought a Denali truck, and Red bought a Durango. Jilla, on the other hand, he had to come out hard. He bought himself a Range Rover. They all put big shiny rims on their whips and threw in hella beats.

After they copped the vehicles, everybody went and parked them in the projects. They were all sitting pretty, lined up right behind one another. They then jumped in Jilla's Range and headed downtown to the Magnificent Mile so that they could do some shopping. Jilla had waited on the day to do this, his game was now stepped up.

They went in and out of designer clothing store after designer clothing store. All living up to the adage, *shop til you drop.*

Finished up with shopping for clothes, the *Bar None* crew then found a jewelry store. One by one, they each put in orders for platinum chains along with custom made, *Bar None,* charms.

Following their jewelry store orders, they ate lunch at Lawry's Steakhouse and then marched to a tattoo parlor. There, they each got *Bar None* tatted on their left forearms, and *R.I.P. Great* on their right forearms.

The last two stops of their shopping spree would be the furniture store and then apartment hunting. Jilla selected the Hyde Park neighborhood, Red chose Beverly, and Colors, along with Dusty, landed in Lansing right next door to one another.

That evening, Jilla called Destiny and informed her that he'd be coming over to get the bag of money he'd given her to hold. That was the bag for him to go see Flaco with. Now it was time for business.

* * * *

As they entered the fire lane of the projects, Camelle was beginning to feel relieved. The last couple of days had been stressful on her young mind and all she wanted to do was see Jilla.

Kim was about to drop her off at home and Camelle saw Cheri standing in front of her house. Since she just lived a couple houses down from her, Camelle told Kim to drop her off right there.

As Camelle got out of Kim's car, she noticed the new line of vehicles parked outside and hoped like hell that Kim didn't. She did though.

"Whose cars are those?" Kim asked Cheri as Camelle was getting out of the car.

"That's Jilla's new truck right there." Cheri responded,

pointing, not knowing anything about what had been happening the last couple of days.

"Yeah?" Kim said suspiciously but not showing it.

"Yeah!" Cheri replied, now pointing at the other cars one by one. "That's Dusty's, that one is Red's, and that one is Colors'. They all got new whips."

Camelle just stood there in silence wishing Cheri would shut her damn mouth. Kim continued to bombard her with question after question. "Damn Cheri, when they get them?" She prodded, faking like she was impressed when actually she was investigating.

"A couple of days ago." Cheri replied. "You should've seen all of them shopping bags they had."

"For real." Kim replied, giving Camelle a look of sarcasm that only the two of them caught. "It looks like your man is doing his thing." she then said to Camelle. Camelle just held her head down and begun playing in the rocks on the ground with her foot.

Kim had heard enough. Her suspicions were now centered solely on Jilla. She told Cheri goodbye and pulled off. Right before she got on the expressway, she sent Camelle a text message as she waited at a red light. "Don't let me find out Jilla got that money."

CHAPTER FIFTEEN

Jilla pulled into the back parking lot of La Exquisita. He didn't know Flaco's telephone number, so he had to do something that he'd rather not, show up unexpectedly. Jilla knew that doing this could cause all types of flags to be raised by Flaco and that it wasn't the proper manner to conduct business in. He was stuck in between a rock and a hard place though, so he had to do what he had to do.

After walking around to the front of the restaurant, Jilla entered the door. Looking around, he noticed a few familiar faces that he'd grown accustomed to seeing from when Great used to bring him along with him. A waitress here, a cook there, then he noticed Julian, Flaco's bodyguard. Jilla immediately began to walk towards him.

"Excuse me Sir, do you have reservations?" Asked the Maître d'.

"No ma'am." Jilla responded. "I just need to speak with him right there." Jilla said, now pointing in the direction of Julian.

"I'm sorry Sir. You need to have reservations to enter into this establishment." The Maître d' informed him.

"Ma'am, I'm good friends with the owner and I need to speak with…"

Before Jilla could finish his sentence, Julian walked up to them.

"Is there some type of problem here Isabelle?" he interrupted.

Julian happened to notice Jilla and her exchanging words and recognized Jilla's face.

"Yes Sir. This guy here said that he needed to speak with you, and I informed him that he needed to have reservations. Jilla was relieved to see Julian.

He never wanted to cause a scene at Flaco's establishment but Jilla needed to see him desperately. Desperate times called for desperate measures, so Jilla knew he would've resorted to anything to see Flaco. Luckily it didn't come to that.

"You did right Isabelle. However, this is a good friend of ours." Julian said as he extended his hand to Jilla.

Jilla extended his as well and they shook.

"Oh, I'm sorry Señor?" Isabelle said, not knowing the name of the mystery man before her eyes.

"Just call me Jilla."

"Oh, okay. I'm sorry Señor Jilla." Isabelle responded with a slight look of embarrassment.

"No need to be sorry. You were just doing your job. You could work at a restaurant of mine anytime. As a matter of fact, I might need you as my personal security someday." Jilla said jokingly.

Once they got into Flaco's office, Julian took a seat behind Flaco's desk and Jilla sat on the couch. Just the sight of the office gave Jilla flashbacks of Great and him sitting on the very same couch.

"So, what brings you to this side of town?" Julian asked Jilla.

"I need to talk to Flaco."

"The weathers been pretty hot," Julian replied, letting Jilla know in code that everything had been shut down because the cops were on to Flaco. "So Flaco felt the need to take a sudden vacation. But, if you leave me a number, I'll pass it on to him and I'm quite sure he'll be delighted to hear from you."

This was not the news that Jilla had anticipated receiving. Flaco was the only one, that he knew of, who could fill the order that he needed to place. He left his cell phone number with Julian and headed back to his truck.

Man I need to find a connect, was all he thought to himself as he rode down the Dan Ryan expressway.

Before Jilla made it back to the spot to bear the bad news to Colors, Dusty, and Red, he decided to stop by Dock's Fish to grab him a fish sandwich with cheese and a Dockberry shake. When he pulled up, his sounds had all of the windows of the strip mall vibrating. All eyes were on him. Backing into a parking spot, Jilla noticed a big body BMW parked next to him. *I like dat,* he said to himself.

When Jilla entered the restaurant, he was waiting in line to place his order. As he waited, he noticed two guys staring at him. *What the fuck these niggaz looking at,* he thought to himself.

"Lil Jilla?" One of the guys blurted out as he stood up and began to approach him. Jilla put his hand in his pocket and gripped the .380 that he had on him.

"Dee?" Jilla replied as he unclutched his pistol. He now recognized the face behind the voice.

"What up lil nigga?" Dee said, as he gave Jilla a gangster hug. Dee used to live down the street from Jilla when he was about seven.

Jilla and Dee's little brother Reggie used to be best friends back then. After they moved, Jilla fell out of contact with them and had never seen them again. "Damn boy, I see you dressed like a heavy, riding like a heavy, shittt, what you moving like a heavy?" Dee inquired, asking the last question

Jilla sized Dee up and noticed that, he too, was looking pretty crispy. He had on a blue Lacoste fisherman's hat, a matching blue Lacoste polo shirt, some Lacoste blue jean shorts, a pair of Lacoste ankle socks, and some Lacoste deck shoes. On his wrist was a platinum Movado watch and around his neck was a platinum chain with a cross attached to it, flooded in diamonds. It was apparent to Jilla that Dee had to be doing something, and that whatever it was, he had to be doing it big.

Looking at the other guy that was with Dee, Jilla's *trust none and suspect all* instincts kicked in. "Shiittt, walk with me while you talk with me." he said to Dee while looking at his guy sideways so that Dee could get the hint.

Jilla placed his order with the cashier, then him and Dee made their way outside. Surprisingly, Dee led Jilla to the pearl white, big body BMW that was parked right next to his truck. *Man, I hope dis nigga can fill my order and he ain't just fronting,* was what Jilla was thinking as he opened the passenger's door to hop into Dee's car.

Once inside, Dee grabbed the blunt of dro' out of the ashtray, fired it up, and took a hit. "So, what you doing?" he asked Jilla handing him the blunt.

"I'm doing a lil somethin'." Jilla responded as he took a pull. "What you doing? You be fuckin' with the coke? "

"That's what I do." responded Dee.

"What the numbers like on that shit?" Jilla shot back.

"For you, seventeen-five. I remember when u was a bad ass lil boy my nigga."

"Okay, okay, I'm feeling that." Jilla responded while nodding his head up and down, "Just give me your number and I'mma check you out later on tonight. I'mma be needing one of those things and if my peoples feelin' it, I'mma be right back at you. I'd rather keep it in the family and fuck with you instead of having to keep going the route I been going." Jilla lied, not wanting Dee to know that he'd hit a lick and was just getting on.

"It's all good boy. Just hit me up when you ready and I'll get at you."

The two of them exchanged numbers and returned inside of the restaurant to pick up their orders. They exchanged a couple of more miscellaneous words, and then hopped in their vehicles going their separate ways. Jilla felt like shit may very well be coming together. A small smile inched its way on his face as he headed to the hood.

* * * *

"Where you at?"

"I'm at the spot. Where you at?"

"I'm about to come up the stairs right now."

Jilla was upstairs, at the spot, cooking and bagging up the key that he'd gotten from Dee. He had only purchased a key because he wanted to see if the customers would like the product.

"Heyy Camelle." Red said as she washed out the Pyrex containers that Jilla had just used.

"Hey y'all!" Camelle responded, not only to Red, but to Jilla, Colors, and Dusty as well.

"What up." Colors said as he chopped and bagged up the work.

"This shit look like butter." Jilla said, while holding up a cookie of hard coke to the light and examining it.

"Hell yeah," Dusty added in. "Plus that shit jumped back like a mufucka."

Camelle stood leaning against the doorway to the kitchen with her arms folded over her chest. Jilla looked up from weighing work on the digital scale and noticed that she was staring at him with eyes that said, *I need to talk to you now!!!*. He caught on to the look and made his way over to her.

"Come here baby." he said, placing his right arm around her neck, hugging her. He then led her to the bedroom and shut the door behind them.

"Now I'm your baby, huh?" Camelle said, plopping down on the bed with her arms still folded.

"Oh, so now you ain't my baby?" Jilla replied, as he pushed her down on the bed, climbed on top of her, and began kissing on her neck.

Camelle pushed him away from her, fighting the tingling sensations that Jilla's lips caused to erupt throughout her body.

"She knows." Camelle said with watery eyes and her bottom lip poked out.

"What you mean, she know?" Jilla responded as he got up off of her. "Who knows what?"

"Kim!! She saw all them new cars lined up when she dropped me off, and Cheri got to running her mouth a million miles an hour, talking about how them was y'all new cars and how she seen y'all with all types of shopping bags and shit."

"So!! They ain't got no proof. I been hustling forever."

"Nigga, you went and bought a Range Rover. She know you ain't been hustling like that."

"Well fuck that bitch. What she going to do?"

"You know she gone run straight to Shotgun and tell."

"And??? That nigga ain't gone do shit. If he even act like he want beef I'm gone give him just what the fuck he looking for."

"What about me Jilla? I think Shotgun gone try and get me ain't he?"

"Shorty, I'm your man right?"

"Yeah."

"And your man a killer right?"

"Yeah. "

"So if he even act like he want to pull it, on *Bar None* I'mma kill that chump ass nigga. So don't even trip." Jilla assured Camelle. "Now come on. Let me take my baby shopping. That'll make you feel better."

Jilla took Camelle to Ford City mall and let her do her. Once she got her a new wardrobe, and a few pieces of mall jewelry, she felt a bit better.

CHAPTER SIXTEEN

A few weeks had passed and the *Bar None* crew quickly became a power to be reckoned with throughout the East-Side of Chicago. Once Jilla began consistently placing big-boy orders with Dee, his crew continued to become solidified. Jilla went to the front of the hood and blessed Demon, Ugly, and Slim. He couldn't leave them out of the equation due to Luke and Rello. Not only that, but once their two cliques merged, they became even stronger. After they got the signature *Bar None* tattoos as well, the whole team was eating and ready for the takeover.

* * * *

"Get y'all bitch asses against the fence!" Jilla spat, as him, Demon, Dusty, and Slim jumped out of his truck. At gunpoint, they held up Chedda and couple of other members from his crew.

Jilla had given them two prior warnings that they had better start shopping with the *Bar None* crew or they would have to shut down their block.

"Didn't I tell y'all that *Bar None* work was the only work getting sold around here?

Chedda had been running a cocaine line on his block for longer than he could remember, and was doing extremely well. Even though Jilla was letting his work go for cheaper prices, Chedda couldn't see himself crossing his connect because he had been dealing with him for so long. He also was the reason that Chedda was holding as much cash as he was. That, plus the fact that Chedda was purchasing his coke soft, and Jilla sold his cooked, were the reasons that he never did start dealing with Jilla. Jilla wasn't trying to hear none of that though.

"You niggaz must think shit a joke, huh?" Jilla said, biting down on his bottom lip. "You see this?" he continued, lifting up the *Bar None* charm on his chain. "This what's happening now. Everything else is old news."

As Jilla gave Chedda and his two guys the speech, Dusty, Demon, and Slim were doing the usual. Relieving them of their possessions.

After he was sure that they were done, Jilla continued, "This block under new management. It's get down or lay down with us."

BAAK! BAAK! BAAK!

Jilla sent three bullets through the side of Chedda's head. Dusty, Demon, and Slim followed suit, leaving the other two guys leaking right beside him.

This was the method of takeover used against the few oddballs who were stuck in their ways of doing things. By choice or by force, *Bar None* was taking over. It was as simple as that.

* * * *

"Bet two-thousand the dice come even, one-thousand on hard six, one-thousand on hard eight, and a thousand I pass." After placing all of his bets, Colors blew on the dice and rolled them.

"Three! Crap out." The table attendant yelled out, scooping up all of the chips that Colors had bet.

" Fuck!!" Colors shouted angrily.

He left the craps table and headed back to his car for the third time. Only this trip wasn't to get any more money, it was to leave. Harrah's casino had become a frequent hang out of his ever since he'd went with his cousin one day and hit for $30,000. Much to his chagrin, he ended up losing it all back, plus $15,000 more within the next few days. This became a very bad habit of his that would ultimately lead to his destruction.

* * * *

"Man fool, remember them twin bitches we met at River Oaks last week?" Demon asked Jilla as they pulled off from making a serve.

"Hell yeah, I remember them hoes. How could I not? Especially the one with them juicy ass lips. She look like she can suck the skin off a dick."

"Well we gone see how they get down tonight. That was them I just got off the phone with and they say all they want is some drink and some green and they ready for whatever."

"Shiittt, line 'em up. That's what we on tonight then." Jilla responded as his phone began to ring.

"What up?" he answered.

"Jilla." Camelle replied crying.

"What up shorty? What's wrong with you?"

"Bad News just put a gun to my head and told me to tell him where you're at."

Bad news was Shotgun's right-hand man. While Shotgun was the hustler, Bad News was the killer. He was the one who kept their crew from being preyed on and surrounded Shotgun with the squad of young gunners.

After hearing this, Jilla figured that Kim must've went and told Shotgun about how he had all of a sudden come up, and they had now figured out that he was the one that had robbed them.

What Shotgun had done to Camelle was a silent message that it was war. It was all good with Jilla though, he figured he'd just knock Shotgun off too and leave a trail of dead bodies in the process as he went through his crew to get to him if he had to.

Hoping he would catch Bad News before he left the projects, Jilla hollered into his phone. "Is he still back there?"

"I don't know. He jumped into a silver Lexus truck with three more dudes and they was riding back and forth around the block."

"I'm on my way back there right now." Jilla said, snapping his phone shut. "Demon, hurry up to the back. Niggaz done upped heaters on my bitch."

Demon punched the gas, letting the Hemi engine of his Chrysler 300 do what it did best, get them where they needed to be as fast as possible.

* * * *

Immediately after dusk, Jilla and Demon stood with their guns drawn as they conversed with Camelle and Red about what had just taken place. All four of them had been riding through the projects as Jilla and Demon hoped to run across the Lexus truck that Camelle told them Bad News was driving. Coming up short, they were now waiting on the rest of the crew to show up.

"Who that right there?" Demon asked, cocking back the hammer of his 9-millimeter. Two minivans with tinted windows were creeping up at a slower than normal driving speed.

Moving to the middle of the fire lane, Jilla raised both of his pistols and aimed at the vans to open fire.

"Whoa, whoa, it's us!" Slim shouted, sticking his head out the sunroof of the first van.

Lowering the gun, as well as the rush of his adrenaline, Jilla tucked one of them into his waistline and kept the other one out and in his hand. Dusty and Ugly parked behind Slim and slid the side door open to the van they were in. "You lucky it was us because you would've been in a world of trouble with all this shit we got." Dusty said, as he showed off the arsenal that was laid out on the back seat of the minivan.

"We can take on a whole police station with this shit." Ugly added.

More than content with what he saw before him, Jilla was ready to go take care of the business. "Y'all seen Colors? I been calling his phone like a mufucka and it keep going straight to voicemail."

"Jilla you know he probably with one of them chicken-head ass bitches. You know it ain't even no use in calling him when he fucking off with one his little sluts." Red shouted from where her and Camelle were standing.

Yeah, or on that mufuckin' casino boat, Jilla thought to himself.

"It's all good. Keep hitting his phone for me. If you get in contact with him while we're gone, just let him know what's going on and tell him to hit my phone." Jilla instructed Red.

"You and Camelle gone and go find some girly shit to get into. Make sure y'all be safe. You got your hammer with you?"

"For sure." Red replied, showing the guys her .32 automatic.

"We'll holler at y'all when we get through *Break Bread* hunting." Jilla finished, as the guys packed into the vans.

Camelle had given them the location of the block that the *Break Bread* clique considered their headquarters. Cranking up the engines, and peeling off, they headed to their destination.

* * * *

YACK! YACK! YACK! YACK! FLACOWI FLACOW! BAAK! BAAK! BAAK! BAAK!

Spat the choppers and automatic weapons.

"*Bar None* bitches!!" Yelled the voices of the ski—masked shooters in the black minivan as they were letting off shots. The members of the *Break Bread* crew were dropping like flies and running for cover.

Pow! Pow! Pow!

A few shots fired back at the van. They were meaningless though because, Slip Knot, the guy shooting them had his eyes closed and had been shot in the leg. He was firing off, hoping it would help get the van full of vengeful shooters up off of their asses.

* * * *

"Did you see them boys' faces when we slid open them doors?" Ugly said, laughing.

"Them boys saw them choppers in they faces and I bet you they shitted on they self." Demon said, sitting down the bottle of Remy he was drinking and grabbing a blunt out of the box so that he could roll some weed.

"Lil Illa, grab that door." Jilla yelled from in the kitchen to the living room.

Lil Illa was Jilla's new little dumper for the spot. Him and his homeboy Gady approached Jilla one day saying they wanted to get some money. When Jilla looked into their eyes, all he saw was him and Colors all over again. He immediately took a liking to them. From that day on, he showed them the ropes and turned the spot over to them.

"Where you been at fool?" Dusty asked Colors as he walked

through the door.

"Taking care of business." Colors responded. "What y'all been on is the question?" Ski-masks and guns were scattered all over the kitchen table.

"While you been chasing hoes, or whatever the fuck you been doing, we been putting in that work firing up them *Break Bread* niggaz." Jilla snapped. "It's on with them bitches every time one of 'em get spotted. That punk mufucka Bad News upped pistol on Camelle talking about, he looking for me. Make sure you spread the word that I got a brick on Shotgun's head. That bitch gotta die."

The guys went on explaining everything that had went down to Colors. As they were talking, Color's cell phone rang. It was his cousin from Terror-Town. His guy, who he used to grab the work from for Jilla, before they robbed Shotgun, wanted to cop two bricks. Colors couldn't fill the order, so he called Jilla into another room.

"What's up?" Jilla asked, exhaling weed smoke into the air.

"Dude and them from the Town need two bricks."

"Well, why you ain't handle it?"

"Cause I can't cover the order."

"What you mean you can't cover the order? I just gave you two soft ones this morning. If you through with them, where the bread at?"

"Naw fool, that's why my phone ain't been on." Colors began explaining. "I ain't want to tell you in front of fam and them but, the dicks got on me earlier and it was Watkins and Davis."

Watkins and Davis were two dirty detectives who had been harassing them ever since their juvenile days.

"And?" Jilla asked.

"They got behind me and threw on they lights. I pulled over and instead of throwing my shit in park, I just put it in neutral. They walked up to the car with they guns pointed at me. As soon as they got up on the car, I threw my shit back in drive and skirted off on them bitches."

"And?"

"They jumped back in they shit and chased a nigga. I was high-speeding for about 30 minutes. Couldn't shake them bitches for shit."

"Well, look like you got away to me, so, what?"

"A, we about to get up outta here. We missing too much money." Demon interrupted, hollering at Jilla.

"Aight, y'all be safe. What about them twin hoes?"

"We gone have to reschedule them. My phone jumping." Demon responded.

"Aight fool, don't bust them hoes down without me though."

"You know I got you gangsta." Demon shot back, as him, Ugly and Slim left out the door.

Jilla then got back to Colors. "Aight, so then what?"

"Man, them bitches was on my ass so hard, I had to end up jumping out and hitting it with my heat and the brick and a half I was finna go serve. I threw that shit and when I went back to get it, after I got away, the shit was gone. "

Jilla doubted Colors' story because he knew that he had developed a gambling habit. However, their bond wouldn't allow him to fully believe that his nigga would beat him out of any money. "So you don't got shit? You trying to tell me that I just lost out on forty-thousand dollars?"

"Naw, I got like thirty-four at the crib for you, but that's it."

Colors had a dude in Grove Heights waiting on him for a brick and a half. He had him give him the money up front but had Jilla thinking otherwise.

Jilla was hot. If Colors was any other normal person, he wouldn't 've shot him right then and there. But seeing how him and Colors grew up like brothers, the love he had for him played in Colors' favor. "Man Colors, you fucking up. You gone have to make this shit up."

"I got you fool. I'm about to straighten you out off of this one score. "

"Aight, come on. First, we boutta go to your crib and grab that bread. Then we can go take care of them cats. "

Colors agreed with no hesitation. Jilla grabbed his heater off of the kitchen table and they left.

CHAPTER SEVENTEEN

"Damn babygirl, thickness is my weakness." Spat a dude from the driver's seat of a money green '78 drop top Impala sitting on 24-inch Davins.

"Who the fuck this nigga talking to?" Red asked her girls as they walked to her truck.

Her, Strawberry, and Passion were just coming from getting their weekly manicures and pedicures.

"Yeah, I'm talking to you lil mamma." The dude in the Impala said, pointing his finger at Red. "What's your name if you don't mind me asking?"

"Who the fuck is this dude?" Red mumbled. All of the girls began giggling.

"I don't know, but he is cute." Passion said, as they got into Red's truck.

"Damn, a mufucka ask you your name and its comedy, huh? "

He is fine, Red thought to herself. Closing the truck door, and rolling the window down, she said, "My name Killa."

"Killa? How you get a name like that?" he asked with a

confused look on his face.

"Cause I keep that killa 'dro." Red responded.

While Jilla had put the rest of the crew down with cocaine, the girls served 'dro.

"Is that right?" he said, as he got out of his car and walked up to the truck.

He immediately saw Red's fat ass pussy print through the white Capri pants she was wearing. It was evident that she wasn't wearing any panties.

As he stood at the door of her Durango, two dudes walked out of Shark's Fish and hopped inside of his car.

"I'm trying to see what's to that 'dro and you at the same time." he said to Red. "That shit do smell fire."

Passion had fired up a blunt which Strawberry was now puffing on. She took a few tokes and passed it to Red.

"Here you go baby. You and your guys can get the rest of this." Red said, handing the blunt to dude after hitting it a few times. "If you feeling it, you can just hit me up and we can take it from there."

The dude grabbed the blunt from Red and began to head back to his car. Just as he was about to open the car door, he thought about something, and turned back around. "Hold on Lil Momma, I don't even got your number."

"I was waiting to see how long it was going to take you to figure that out." Red said, as her, Passion, and Strawberry began giggling again.

"Jokes on me today, I guess." he said. "A, just give me your phone and I'll call mines. That way we'll have each other's numbers."

Red grabbed her phone from inside the cup holder and

handed it to him. He dialed up his cell phone, and as soon as it started ringing, hit the end button. Handing Red her phone back, he said, "That's me right there, baby."

"Okay, and... What am I supposed to put, Mystery Man for your name?"

Passion and Strawberry, again, began giggling.

"Damn, your fine ass got me tripping like a mufucka. My name Money sweetheart."

Red then began putting his name in her phone. As he got one last look at her, he couldn't help but notice her cleavage due to the low-cut shirt she was wearing. Even though she had perfect breast, it wasn't them that caught his attention. It was the charm on her chain and the tattoo on her forearm that made him all the more determined to get inside her pants.

****

After going to Colors' house to get the money, him and Jilla shot to Jilla's crib to cook up the coke. Colors stretched the two bricks into three and a half. After that, they jumped into Colors' Denali and headed to take care of the business.

When they pulled into the parking lot of Kentucky Fried Chicken, Colors dialed up his cousin's cell phone.

"What up?" Colors' cousin answered.

"Where y'all at?" Colors asked.

"We here, where y'all at?"

"We here too."

Looking around, Colors' cousin spotted Colors' truck. "I see y'all. We right here in the blue Avalanche truck."

"Oh, okay, I see y'all." Colors said, as he backed into the parking spot beside them.

Jilla had a .40 cal. on his lap and was emptying the tobacco out of a blunt wrap, into the ashtray.

Colors tucked his 9-millimeter in his waistline and hopped out the car with a Walgreen's bag that had the two bricks in it. He opened the back door to the Avalanche and hopped in.

When Colors hopped into the Avalanche, the interior light came on allowing Jilla to catch a glimpse of the dude in the driver's seat.

Damn, I know that nigga from somewhere, he thought to himself.

After he was done serving the dudes, Colors jumped back in his truck and threw the bag of money on Jilla's lap. "That's forty-five right there, we even. I'm about to front this other one to one of my other guys but I'mma need two more to keep trapping with."

One thing about Colors was, no matter how much money he messed up, he knew how to maneuver and get right back so that he could pay Jilla off. If gambling didn't have such a grip on him, the sky would be the limit with him. He knew how to move that work.

"Yeah, I see you Mr. Get Back." Jilla said, licking the blunt. "But, aye, who was that driving that Avalanche?" he questioned, pushing in the cigarette lighter.

"That's my cousin's guy. He the one that was straightening us out after them bitch ass niggaz killed Great."

"Yeaahh? I know him from somewhere. What's his name?"

"They call him Y.B."

"Y.B.!! Get the fuck outta here!"

" Straight up. Why? What up?"

"Me, Great, Luke, and Rello did that boy real dirty one night. We found out he was cheating me on the dice and lifted him for all his jewelry and bread. We left his pretty ass buck naked in an alley."

They both started laughing. "On *Bar None*?" Colors asked.

"Hell yeah, on *Bar None*. He laid some t's down on me and hit me for like four or five racks."

"Whaatt..."

"It's a small ass mufuckin world ain't it?"

They both rode off still laughing. Who would've ever thought that Y.B. would be getting fed by Jilla or vice versa, and neither one of them even knew it?????

* * * *

"What' up?" Dee greeted Jilla as he entered his apartment. Dee was the only one besides the members of the *Bar None* crew that Jilla trusted with knowing where he laid his head. "I gotta piss like a mufucka. Let me use your bathroom."

"You gotta hold up a minute. My girl in there taking a shower. Jilla had moved Camelle in with him after what Bad News had pulled on her.

They walked into the kitchen where Jilla had $175,000 neatly stacked on the table. Dee sat the backpack, with the ten bricks in them, on the kitchen counter. He then unloaded them and replaced them with the money.

"You doing good youngster." Dee said to Jilla. Out the corner of his eye, he saw Camelle coming out of the bathroom and going into the bedroom with nothing but a bath towel wrapped around her. *Damn shorty thick as hell,* he thought to himself.

Jilla was grabbing two bottled waters out of the refrigerator when he heard the bedroom door close. "I'm just trying to catch up with you." he replied. "A, you can gone and use that bathroom now. Shorty done."

Dee went to use the bathroom and then returned to the kitchen. "Man Jilla." Dee said as he grabbed his bottled water off of the table. "You know I keep my ear to the streets, and I been hearing your name ringing like a motherfucker." He then unscrewed the top off the bottle and took a swig. "You gots to be cool with all that shoot 'em up bang bang shit. Getting money and gang banging don't mix."

Jilla got offended when he told him that. He felt like Dee was trying to scold him. "That's how I get down." Jilla spat with his face frowned up, looking Dee up and down. "How you think I been bringing you all this bread? From putting in work and taking over shit." he finished.

"Aight boy. Calm down. I 'm just letting you know that's how you make yourself hot."

"Just let me do me. As long as I'm pitching this work, that's all you need to worry about."

In Jilla's eyes, Dee was soft. As much as the guys persisted on trying to persuade Jilla to rob Dee, Jilla never conceded to their wishes. Dee was helping Jilla eat and he was loyal to him based on that. But if Dee got in the habit of throwing shade at him, Jilla hoped that he understood that all of that loyalty could go out of the window in the blink of an eye.

CHAPTER EIGHTEEN

"Man look, ain't that Slim's maxima right there?" Slip Knot asked, as he was about to turn into the parking lot of the liquor store on Stoney Island.

"Ooh wee, it shole the fuck is." Bad News responded. "Keep going and park around the corner. I got this nigga." he continued as he checked his pistol to make sure it was a bullet in the chamber.

After Slip Knot pulled around the corner and parked, he wished like hell that he could go and take care of the business with Bad News. But the gunshot wound to his leg still hadn't healed up.

Bad News slid his hoodie over his head and got out the car. As he approached Slim's Maxima, he noticed that he wasn't alone. It was another person in the car with him.

"Here goes my Beanie Siegal C.D. " Dusty said to Slim. "You and Jilla always cuffing my shit. I been looking all over for this mufucka.

BAAK! BAAK! BAAK!

Bad News crept up on the car and got to unloading through

the driver's side window. Instantly Slim clutched his stomach and tried ducking for cover.

BAAK! BAAK! BAAK! BAAK!

As Dusty attempted to open the passenger side door Bad News flooded him with three shots in the back and one in his top right shoulder.

FLACOW! FLACOW! FLACOW!

Dusty fired back over his shoulder, not looking where he was shooting. The returned gunfire forced Bad News to stand down in an effort to take cover.

Hearing the gunshots from inside the store, Ugly left the liquor on top of the checkout counter, and sprinted outside. As he made his way through the exit door, he noticed Slim's Maxima riddled with bullet holes and a dude with a black hoodie on running away from the scene.

YACK! YACK! YACK! YACK!

Ugly shot, as he attempted to chase down Bad News. He couldn't chase him too far though because Slim was laid out on the ground, bleeding like a hog, and Dusty was slumped over in the driver's seat of the Maxima.

"Pull off nigga!! Hurry up!" Bad News yelled, as he jumped into the car with Slip Knot.

Skirrrrr...

Slip Knot's grey Shelby GT Ford Mustang peeled out. "Did you get them?" Slip Knot asked in a frantic tone.

"Do a bear shit in the woods and wipe his ass with a white rabbit?" Bad News quipped. They both started laughing. "I got Dusty's lil bitch ass and Slim." Bad News bragged, as he took off his hoodie and threw it in the back seat.

"Damn nigga!! We ain't even get our drank first so how we gone celebrate?" Slip Knot jokingly asked.

"Shoot up to 75th. We can hit the liquor store up their then ride down on Shotgun and let him know the good news. He gone wig out when he hear this."

* * * *

The area was smokey and bells were ringing. Nervous gamblers lit up cigarette after cigarette as various slot machines chimed signaling off big hits for lucky winners. Card tables were filled to capacity, while crap tables were getting big stakes bet at them.

In the midst of it all, Colors found himself, once again, victimized by the monster. This time, he didn't just gamble away a portion of Jilla's money, he lost all of it. Colors was officially flat broke. He'd lost a record breaking $56, 000.

Making his way to his car, with his head hung low, his brain was working overtime. Damn, how the fuck I'm finna get Jilla's money? He thought to himself.

* * * *

Red and Money were downtown at the Four Seasons Hotel. After purchasing a few pounds of 'dro from her, he had opened the door for a few sessions of casual conversation. A few purchases, and charismatic conversations, later, he found himself where he had been so determined to get with Red once again.

The candle lit dinner at Carmines, horse and carriage ride, hand in hand walk on the lakefront, and rose petaled path to the hotel bed, more than made his mission all the more accomplishable. Red had never been romanced in such fashion.

Two bottles of Rose Moet sat in the bucket, on chill, as the flickering flames from the fireplace accentuated the dimly lit room. Oozing through the speakers at just above a whisper, were the mood setting tunes of Musiq Soulchild.

Red had made up her mind that tonight would be the night she'd release all of the pent-up tension that had built up in her since Great's death. It had been a long time now. She was about to show Money how she got down.

After getting out of the shower, Red emerged from the bathroom. Her hair was wet and slicked back. Wrapped around her body was a thick, white, terry clothed bath towel that stopped at the curve of her Trina like ass. Money could see it jiggling while looking at her from the front.

Looking into his eyes, she dropped the towel to the floor. Her body was coated with a thin layer of moisture which lingered from the shower she'd just taken. The flames from the fireplace reflected off of her, causing her entire body to glisten.

Money was seated in a velour arm-chair. He was clad in only a pair of Sean John boxers. As he was rolling a blunt of 'dro, *Big Booty Hoes #11* played on the television.

"Viola." Red said, as she spun around in a circle on the balls of her feet with her arms extended away from her side. "You made me feel good today, so, in return, now I'm going to make you feel good." she said, after she completed her 360-degree spin and began walking towards him.

I'm about to tear this pussy up, Money thought to himself as Red seductively headed his way. With an ear to ear smile, he lit up the blunt, took a pull, and asked, "How you plan on doing that?"

Just the sight of her had his soldier standing up at full attention.

Red walked up to him and got so close that she could feel Money's hot breath tickling her stomach. She then got down on her knees and eased his boxers off of him. Throwing them to the side with her left hand, she began stroking his manhood with her right.

"Just sit back and relax, enjoy the ride." she purred.

Money threw his head back and took a couple more tokes off of the blunt. The feeling of Red's soft hand caressing him sent shivers of delight through him as the blunt of 'dro heightened the sensitivity of his body.

Noticing the pre-cum beginning to crinkle out of him, she traced her tongue around the entire base of his pole. Red then licked the pre-cum off of it like it was the caramel topping of an ice cream cone.

"Damn girl, that shit feel good as hell." Money complimented as he held on to the arms of the chair with a tight grip.

"Does it daddy?" she replied, placing him inside of her mouth. Red then began sucking him in a slow and methodical manner.

The warmness of her saliva sent him into a state of euphoria. "Shit shorty!" Money shouted, as his toes curled up and dug into the plushness of the carpet beneath them.

Red then began sucking him faster and faster while rolling his balls around with her free hand. "You like... that?" she asked in between sucks, as she attacked his stick like a state-of-the-art pro.

Little did he know; he was being pleasured so well because Red's full-time profession used to be satisfying men.

"Hell... yeah... I... like... that shit." Money responded in between pants. He now had his hand on the back of her head. Red deep throated him deeper and deeper making slurping and popping sounds with her mouth.

"Shit, I'm about to nut!" Money warned her. Red Sucked harder and faster as she used her fee hand to rub on her own love box.

"Here it come, here it come!" Money grunted.

Surprising to him, Red didn't release the tight grip her mouth had on him. She just rubbed her clit at a faster pace and continued sucking.

"Oooh shit." Money said, as he released his load into her mouth. Red took all of it in as she simultaneously brought herself to a climax as well. As they both came, she kept on sucking him, making sure she didn't allow him to become limp.

After seeing that she'd gotten him back as hard as he could get, Red stood up and placed each of her feet in the chair, on the outside of Money's thighs. She then reached down, grabbed his dick, and guided it inside of her.

"Oooh...." Red moaned. It had been so long since she felt a man inside of her, she'd forgotten just how good it felt.

"Damn, yo' shit tight as hell." Money grunted.

Biting down on her bottom lip, Red eased up and down slowly, allowing Money to enter deeper into her, inch by inch with each stroke. Her love box was as wet as wet could be. After she adjusted to his thickness, she took him to the promised land riding him cowgirl style.

Once they both came again, Money led her to the bed. "My turn now. Get on your hands and knees."

Many more positions later, after they both took turns pleasuring one another, they passed out in each other's arms drained of all their bodily fluids.

* * * *

The emergency room of Trinity Hospital was packed, as usual. Ugly called the rest of the crew, letting them know what had went down. His clothes and hands were soaked in blood from helping Slim out of the car.

After chasing the unknown assailant away, he had run back to the car and noticed that Slim's intestines were hanging out of his stomach. Pulling him out of the car, he laid Slim on the ground, and pushed his intestines back in with his bare hands. While he was tending to Slim, a miscellaneous woman, that was inside the liquor store, was on the other side of the car tending to Dusty until the paramedics arrived.

It seemed like everyone who was inside of the emergency room was looking at Ugly. He had so much blood on him that it looked as if he had himself killed someone. 'What the fuck all these mufuckaz lookin' at?' He thought to himself. Feeling uncomfortable, he got up and went into the concessions area to grab a Red Bull.

* * * *

Jilla and Demon marched into the emergency room with a couple of chicks, who happened to be riding with them when they got the call, in tow. As they approached the check in counter, the receptionist had her back to them filing papers into a cabinet.

"Excuse me." Jilla approached her.

She swiveled around in her chair and looked at him over her glasses. "How can I help you?"

"Yeah, we lookin' for Arthur Woods and James Smith." Jilla informed her, giving the alias names that Ugly had told him Slim and Dusty were checked in under.

"Okay, let me see." the receptionist said as she began pecking on the keyboard of her computer. Shaking her head, she looked back up and removed her glasses, leaving them dangling from the string that they were attached to. "I think you need to speak with the doctor." She picked up the phone and, just as she was about to page him, spotted the doctor. "As a matter of fact, there he is right there." she said pointing towards the concessions area.

He was talking to Ugly.

"What's the deal Ugly?" Demon asked as him and Jilla walked up. The two girls had taken a seat in the emergency room waiting area.

"Yeah, what's up with fool and them?" Jilla asked Ugly as well while at the same time sizing up the doctor.

He was a short, thin, clean cut Hindu guy in his mid-forties, wearing a pair of thick bifocal type glasses. In his left hand he had two sets of charts.

"Man, this nigga talkin' some bull shit." Ugly responded while pointing his finger in the doctor's face. "I'mma let him tell y'all what he just told me."

"What he talkin' about doc?" Jilla asked, piercing him with angry eyes.

"Yeah, what he talkin' about?" Demon repeated with just as angry eyes.

The doctor took a deep, dry, swallow and thought of the best way to deliver the news to them. Even though he'd done it a million times, bearing bad news had never become an easy thing for him to do. "Well, as I told this young man here." he said, with his heavy accent. "Mr. woods, He continued, referring to Dusty. "One of the bullets that he was hit with struck his spinal cord. The surgery we performed has been successful in removing the bullets from him but I'm afraid that it looks like he'll be paralyzed from the waist down."

"What!!!" Jilla shouted, catching the attention of almost all of the emergency room waiting area occupants.

"Get the fuck outta here!" Demon added. "What about Slim?"

"I'm assuming you re referring to Mr. Smith." the doctor replied, trying to figure out how to deliver the words that were about to come out of his mouth. "I'm sorry to have to inform you of this, but Mr. Smith was pronounced D. O. A. He lost too much blood before the paramedics were able to make it to him."

* * * *

Red's cell phone vibrated on the stand that was next to the bed in the hotel room. She figured it was one of her customers calling because they wanted some 'dro. Looking over at Money, who was still passed out asleep, she thought to herself, *I just might be able to make him my man.* As she grabbed her phone, and looked at the caller I.D., she noticed that it was Strawberry.

"Hellooo." Red teasingly answered.

"Where you at girl?" Passion questioned. Her and Strawberry were calling on a three-way.

"None of your business." she playfully replied, snaking her neck even though the girls couldn't see her.

"Bitch, Dusty and Slim just got shot up at the liquor store on Stoney Island. They at Trinity. Everybody on their way up there right now." Strawberry informed her.

"Shit!! I'm on my way up there right now." Red hollered and hung up her phone.

Money jumped up out of his sleep looking startled. "What up shorty? What's wrong?" he asked, wiping the slob from the corner of his mouth.

"Nothing. I just gotta go take care of some business. " Red responded as she stepped into her thong.

"Is you straight?" he asked, resting himself on one elbow.

"Yeah, I'm good." Red responded, buttoning up her jeans.

"You sure you don't need me to go with you?"

"Naw, I got it. I'll call you later." Red slid her other pump on and rushed out of the hotel room door. *It's always something* she thought to herself.

CHAPTER NINETEEN

Leaving the Casino, Colors was in thirst mode. Noticing that his tank was on empty, he pulled into the shell gas station and remembered that he didn't have any money to even purchase the gas. Luckily Michelle, Demon's sister, was with him. She had to give him the $20 to put into his gas tank.

After paying for the gas, he was heading out the door wondering just how it was that he could hit his next lick. He had to hit one because he had to pay Jilla.

"Colors?" he heard someone say, breaking him out of his train of thought.

"Dimp?" Colors responded.

Dimp was a light-skinned chubby dude with freckles and dimples. That's how he got his name. He grew up in the Jeffery Manor as well, but after leaving the hood to go up to the state capital of Springfield, Illinois with one of the guys named Low, he got busted in a drug raid by the D. E. A. The word. on the street was that he ended up testifying against Low and Low got sentenced to 45 years of Fed time just off of Dimp's testimony.

In return for his cooperation, Dimp ended up getting out in 5 years. After attempting to return to the hood, Dimp had gotten shade threw at him from everybody he tried to associate with. He'd been shot a couple of times and quickly got the message that he was no longer welcomed in the hood. After that happened, he moved and no one else had heard from him or seen him since.

"Yeah nigga. What up with you boy?" Dimp replied.

" Shiitt fool, you know me, just chillin' and shit. " Colors rebutted, looking around. He'd never want anyone from the hood to happen to see him associating with Dimp.

"I see you looking good. That must mean you doing good too, huh?" Dimp said, hitting Colors with lines, trying to butter him up.

"Naw, I'm just chillin' and shit. Working for the construction company." Colors lied.

"Aww man, there you go." Dimp replied while throwing his hands in the air and then letting them fall back down to his side. "I know that shit was fucked up with what happened with me and Low. But I was facing life my nigga."

"That's the oldest trick in the book boy. The Feds throw I big ass football numbers in your face and instantly they make weak mufuckaz fold. You think they would 've dropped your shit from life all the way down to five years just for telling on Low? They pimped you."

"I feel you my nigga. If I could do that shit all over again I would 've just took my hit like a G. My conscious fuck with me all the time behind that shit. I wouldn't ever go like that again."

"From the looks of things, you done jumped right back down again too."

"Boyy, I'm up in Indiana killing 'em. I just can't find a consistent connect."

"What you doing up there?" Colors asked, one eyebrow raised.

"I 'm pitching Chicago dimes for thirty bucks a pop nigga. It's super sweet up there." Dimp replied with a smile.

"Yeah?? So what you playing with?" Colors asked him.

"I'm fucking with about two to three bricks at a time but them Indiana cats be taxing the shit out of me."

"What they charging you?"

"Nigga, they hitting me in the head for 27 a brick. Hard at that, and that shit be garbage. "

"Whaaattt?" Colors responded, seeing the door open for him to hit the lick he had been in search for.

"Yeah fool, and I 'm moving like 8 to 10 a week for them chumps."

The wheels inside of Colors' head immediately got to turning. He knew that fucking with Dimp was taboo, but the numbers he was talking were sounding beautiful. That, plus the sincerity his voice seemed to be filled with while he was giving his *I regret that shit* speech, along with the fact that the casino had just left him broke, made him go against his better judgement.

"I tell you what, Dimp. Like I told you, I ain't even getting down no more." Colors said as he removed his cell phone from his hip and looked around again. "But I know somebody that'll probably be able to beat that number and take care of you for 25 a brick, hard. And it'll be some butter."

"Hell yeah, fool. That's what I need. I'll probably shoot up to moving 15 a week if it's butter like that.

"Aight, say no more. Put my number in your phone and hit me up tomorrow. I'mma get up with my dude and get you right."

They exchanged numbers and went their separate ways. After Colors pumped his gas, and was just about to pull out of the gas station, Dimp pulled up next to him in a grey dodge charger sitting on 24's. He honked his horn and threw up a balled-up fist to Colors as if signaling Black Power. *He just might be doing alright* Colors thought to himself. He threw the balled-up fist back up to him and pulled off.

"Wasn't that Dimp?" Michelle asked, looking at Colors crazy.

"Yeah, that was his bitch ass." Colors replied.

"I hope you don't trust him." she said, knowing Dimp was bad business.

"Hell naw!!" Colors lied. "You know that nigga work with them people."

His cell phone then rang, interrupting their conversation.

It was Jilla informing him about what had happened to Slim and Dusty.

"Whaatt!! I'm on my way." Colors responded. He then went and dropped Michelle off at home and sped to the hospital.

* * * *

"Slim dead and Dusty laid up in the mufuckin hospital." Jilla snapped as he banged his fists on the kitchen table. I can't believe this shit." he continued as he stood up and kicked the side of the refrigerator.

The *Bar None* crew was all sitting around the kitchen table at the spot. Weed, guns, pop cans being used for ashtrays, and liquor bottles were scattered all over. While Jilla was venting his anger, Demon was transfixed on a roach that was crawling along the faucet on the sink.

"You know what nigga?" Demon stood up and said, putting his cigarette out on top of a Code Red Mountain Dew can. "Sitting here doing all this pouting ain't gone do a mufuckin thing."

"Hell mufuckin naw. Let's go wet them bitches block up again." Colors said.

"Yeah, make them hoe ass niggaz feel the pain every time they step foot out on they shit." added Ugly.

"Fuck that!!" Jilla hollered out as he grabbed his gun off of the table. He turned up the quart of Hennessy, took a few gulps, and slammed the bottle back down on the table. "All this back and forth shit ain't about nothing." he spat as he wiped his mouth with the back of his hand. "I don't want nobody but Shotgun now. And I know just how to get him."

* * * *

The sun had set and the night had brought the perfect setting

for what was set to take place. Colors and Ugly sat on 117 &
State, inside of Ugly's Monte Carlo. Even though the car was
filled with 'dro smoke, and they were parked two blocks away,
they could still observe the block with the help of the two sets
of high-powered night vision binoculars they'd purchased from
Sportmart. They could've easily shot up or killed any of the
various soldiers from the *Break Bread* crew but none of them
were the intended targets. It was Shotgun or nothing tonight.

Slipknot was out on the block, crutches and all, running the
operation. He was directing traffic, collecting money from
workers, and re-handing out packs.

"Look how easy we could get this goofy." Colors said as he
refocused the vision on his binoculars and beamed down on
Slipknot.

"I know my nigga. " Ugly replied as he handed Colors a
blunt.

"These bitch ass boys just got down on us yesterday and
they ain't even got they security tight. They ain't respecting our
gangster."

"Hell naw, fuck all this waiting shit. I say we just go kill
every single one of them bitches." Colors said, pointing at the
various guys that were posted up on the block. "Look at 'em,
they sitting ducks."

Just as Colors finished saying that, a fuchsia colored
Porsche Cayenne truck pulled onto 119th and stopped in the
middle of the street.

"Look!! There go the Porsche truck." Ugly blurted out,
while fumbling to unclip his cell phone from his hip with his
free hand.

"Shole the fuck is." Colors replied, as he stayed focused on the truck.

The Cayenne pulled into the street and stopped in the middle of the block. Slipknot made his way up to the truck and handed a filled-up shopping bag through the window. The passenger retrieved the bag from him, and handed another filled up one to him in return. It was evident that a pickup and drop off was going down.

Jilla had informed Colors and Ugly on what types of vehicles to be on the lookout for. "I've seen him in three different cars." Jilla recalled Camelle telling him when he had drilled her for all of the information that he could about Shotgun. "A purplish like Porsche truck, a black Jaguar, and a burgundy Harley Davidson truck."

He relayed that information to Ugly and Colors and instructed them to chirp him as soon as they spotted any of those vehicles.

* * * *

Demon and Jilla sat in the back seats of the stolen Suburban truck, behind the tints. They were parked southward on Wentworth Street. In the driver and passenger seats sat Red and Passion.

As the four waited patiently inside of the truck, they passed 'dro blunt after 'dro blunt around. Demon and Jilla vibed to Beanie Siegel's, *'I Can Feel It In The Air'*, as Red and Passion gossiped on the phone with Strawberry. She was telling them how she'd just tricked some cat in a Benz to pay her rent.

Beep, beep... Beep beep... Jilla's chirper sounded off "Yeah." he spoke into his phone as he reached and turned the volume down on the c.d. player.

"He on the block." Ugly whispered into his chirper with urgency. He was so caught up in the moment that he was whispering as if the guys on the block could actually hear him.

"Red, let's go." Jilla said as he simultaneously snapped his fingers twice and sat up in his seat. "Get y'all asses off of that phone."

"Aight girl, gotta go, bye." Red hurriedly told Strawberry and quickly ended the call. She and Passion then flipped down their sun visors, using the mirrors inside of them to doll up their faces, and made sure their hair wasn't out of place.

Demon reached between his legs and grabbed his automatic .357 Sig Sauer. He pressed the clip release button, ejecting the magazine into his left hand, and checked to make sure that it was filled to capacity with the hollow point Black Rhino's. He then reinserted the clip and made sure it was still one in the chamber.

"He pulling off and coming y'all way now." Ugly's voice blared through the speaker of Jilla's chirper. Only this time he was hollering at the top of his lungs instead of whispering.

Satisfied with her appearance, Red flipped up her sunvisor and started up the truck. "Let's do it bitch." she said to Passion. Passion then flipped her sunvisor back up as well and stuffed her lip gloss back into her handbag.

Approximately seven seconds later, the Porsche truck pulled up to the stop sign at the end of the block. After signaling left, with its blinker, it turned northbound on Wentworth street.

"Damn bust a u!!" Jilla shouted. Red threw the truck in drive and flipped a U-turn.

Catching up to the truck, Red waited until they passed 103rd street and, BOOM! She crashed into the back of it while it was stopped at a stop sign. She then opened the door to the Suburban jumped out, and went into her spill.

"Oh my God, I'm sorry." she screamed hysterically as she walked around to the front of the truck.

Shotgun and Bad News got out of the Cayenne at the same time and made their way around the back of it to see what type of damage had been done.

"Ooh wee. We got both of these niggaz at the same time." Jilla said to Demon, as he pulled the ski-mask over his face.

"Damn baby girl. What's wrong with you? You can't drive or something?" Bad News barked as he looked at the dent in the bumper and the broken taillight.

"I'm sorry. The fire fell off of my blunt and I tried to knock it off of my pants before it burned me. " Red replied.

"Ooh bitch. Rocky gone kill yo' ass. " Passion said, as she made her way around to the front of the Suburban as well, and pointed to the dent in the font of its bumper.

"I know." Red pouted, as she bent down to pick up a piece of the broken headlight that was on the ground. "He gone kick my mufuckin ass. "

Damn this bitch got a fat ass. Shotgun thought to himself as he looked at Bad News to see if he was enjoying the view that he was.

"Look sweetheart, calm down and don't panic." Shotgun

said as he reached inside his jacket to pull out his cell phone. "My guy got a 24-hour auto repair shop and he can have both of our shit fixed in a couple of hours."

"You got it like that?" Red responded, appearing to be relieved.

Damn, a fat ass and a pretty face. Shotgun thought to himself as he looked into her eyes. Bad News had his sights set on Passion, thinking about all the different ways he would love to bend her up and make her cum.

"Look at these sucka for love ass niggaz." Jilla said to Demon, in a calm manner, with a grin on his face.

"That's the power of the pussy my nigga." Demon replied, as he now pulled his mask down over his face.

Red grabbed Shotgun's hand and led him over to the back of his truck. Leaning her back against it, she threw her arms around his neck and whispered into his free ear. "I wanna suck on yo' dick, nonstop, while they fixing our shit. Just to show my appreciation."

Shotgun got to stuttering through the phone to the mechanic as he glanced over at Passion who was grabbing Bad News' manhood.

"Don't neither one of you pussy motherfuckers turn around. Demon spat through clenched teeth as he and Jilla approached. Red had given them a silent signal by throwing up the *Bar None* sign while hugging Shotgun.

Bad News then tried to reach for his gun. Not seeing Jilla easing up behind him, he felt a piece of cold steel pressed against the back of his head.

"Unh, unh playboy. You slow." Jilla stopped him. Get them mufuckin hands in the air and get y'all asses on the ground."

As Jilla and Demon held Shotgun and Bad News at gunpoint, Red and Passion began patting them down. After relieving them of their firearms, the girls bound their wrists and ankles in haste, using duct tape.

As if on cue, Colors and Ugly pulled up and helped throw Shotgun and Bad News in the back of the Suburban.

"Take the truck and burn it." Jilla said to Colors, as he pointed at Shotgun's Cayenne. "Then meet us at you know where."

Instead of taking the truck somewhere and burning it like Jilla told him to, Colors drove and parked it in his garage. After doing business with Dimp a couple of times, Colors remembered him saying something about knowing someone who ran a chop shop in Indiana.

* * * *

Shotgun and Bad News were tied to two separate trees, next to one another. Jilla had gotten two fiends to dig holes for their bodies, approximately eighteen feet away from the trees.

"Y'all must've thought we was soft." Jilla said, as he hurled a brick at Bad News. Him, Demon, and Colors had been stoning Shotgun and Bad News for the past hour.

Shotgun continuously attempted to murmur something despite the fact that his mouth was gagged. His words were indistinguishable though.

"Ha, ha, ha, ha." Jilla laughed, as he turned up the bottle of Cognac, watching Shotgun and Bad News getting brick after brick thrown at them. Ever since Slim's death, and Dusty's paralyzation, he'd begun drinking heavily. "Hold up!!" He shouted with his hand in the air just as Demon was about to throw another brick. "Let's see what these pussy mufuckaz got to say."

Jilla then walked up to each of them, snatched the tape from over their mouths, and removed the gags.

"P... p... please man." cried Shotgun. He and Bad News both had their entire bodies filled with deep gash wounds as blood oozed out of each one of them continuously. Their faces, heads, and lips were swollen like they 'd been beaten with baseball bats.

"Please what bitch!" barked Ugly, as he slung another brick into Shotgun's face from point blank range.

Demon stood there staring down Bad News who hadn't uttered one word of plea.

"Please man, I'm sorry. You can have every penny I got. I'm a millionaire. I'll give it all to you. Just... please... let us go." Shotgun pled in-between whimpers.

Jilla turned up the Cognac again, then slang the empty bottle into Bad News' chest. "This ain't about money." he said, going back and forth, staring both of them down with bloodshot eyes. "This mufucka here." he continued, pointing his finger into Bad News' face. "He killed one of my gangsters and he paralyzed the other. Both at your command. You think money can replace that shit there?"

"Man fuck y'all." Bad News grumbled and then spat a wad of bloody spit into Demon's face.

"Ha, ha." Demon laughed, "I like that. Tough to the grave." He then wiped the spit from his face with the back of his hand and pulled his pistol from his waist. He began beating Bad

News upside the head with it unmercifully.

This motherfucker ain't crying, or whining, or shit. Colors thought to himself. Bad News was taking the torture like a true soldier.

Reds Durango pulled up into the prairie. After she parked, Colors and Ugly went to the truck and helped the girls.

"Damn bitch, we should've put on some gym shoes." Red said to Passion. Walking through the dirt, rocks, and grass was a challenge for them in the pumps that they were wearing.

"I know girl... Ewww, look at these niggaz." Passion whispered to Red as they walked up on the torturing. Her stomach immediately became queasy, feeling like she was about to vomit from looking at the sight of Bad News and Shotgun

"Alas, the man of the hour, " Jilla announced as Ugly and Colors wheeled Dusty over to where they were. Sitting in his lap was an S. K. S. "Here they go fool. Delivered First-Class. You know what Tupac say, *revenge is like the sweetest joy next to getting pussy.*"

Dusty took one last puff off of his Newport cigarette and flicked the butt to the ground. Exhaling the smoke into the air he picked the Japanese weapon off of his lap, and looked both Shotgun and Bad News into their eyes. After locking the wheels on his wheelchair, he emptied the entire 150 round drum into both of their bodies.

"Damn lil nigga, you ain't even say shit before you aired them chumps out." Colors said as he wheeled dusty back to the Durango.

"Ain't shit to be said." he replied as he lit up another cigarette. "The talking went out the window a long time ago."

* * * *

Saturday night the *Bar None* crew decided to go pop bottles and make it rain at Red's no. 5 nightclub. The outing was the celebration of Shotgun and Bad News' departure from God's green earth.

"I don't like that nigga." Demon said to Jilla as he glanced down at the dance floor from the V. I. P. section.

Red and Money were dancing, and Red seemed to be enjoying herself more than Jilla had ever seen her do since Great's death. "I ain't really feeling that goofy either." Jilla rebutted. "But Red seem like she vibing with him, and he been bringing her a lot of bread, so he get a pass for now."

Colors was at the bar mackin' down an Asian looking chick and Ugly was all in the ear of some Latina Mamí.

"Well I don't know about you, but he coming out the gate with two strikes from me. It's just something about the boy that I don't like. " Demon persisted.

"Don't let me find out you got a thang for Red." Jilla said as he tapped Demon on the chest with the back of his left hand.

"Hell naw! That's family fool. You know I can't go like that." Demon responded defensively.

"It's good fool. Relax, this is a night of celebration, if it come, we'll celebrate again. Only it'll be on his behalf." Jilla said and then stood up. Putting his glass down, he then said. "For now though, let's go mingle with some of these pretty ladies and get our party on."

They then went over to where Dusty was, who was surrounded by strippers, and got to making it rain. Shaking up bottles of Kris' and splashing them all over the crowd, they celebrated. *Bar None* style.

CHAPTER TWENTY

Colors sat in the parking lot of BP gas station talking to the Brazilian chick that was in his passenger's seat. He had been fucking on her all night long and decided to take her with him and show her off while he took care of business

Dimp's Charger pulled up next to him and Colors excused himself from her. He grabbed the Macy's bag from the back seat, hopped out of his truck, and made his way over to Dimp's car.

Getting in, and closing the door behind him, Colors said, "Damn fool, what took you so long?"

"My bad fam. I had to drop off this little cutie pie I was fuckin' with last night. " He replied as he reached in his back seat for a backpack. He had on a long-sleeved button up shirt and was sweating profusely.

"Man boy, you sweating like a motherfucker ain't you? Colors asked as he opened the Macy's bag to retrieve one of the cooked-up bricks.

"I been up popping pills and fucking all night fool. I ain't been to sleep yet." Dimp replied as he placed the backpack full of money in-between him and Colors.

"You need to slow down Playboy." Colors replied, "But hey, look at this shit. Straight butter." he bragged.

"I know." Dimp replied, grabbing the cooked-up brick out of Colors' hand. "Since I been copping my coke from you my clientele done shot up like a motherfucker. What's this, like forty-five keys I done bought from you now?

"Yeah, something like that." Colors responded. He really wasn't listening to none of what Dimp was talking about. He just wanted to hurry up and get the money so he could get to the casino.

"You gone have to drop the price for your boy a little. You see how I'm moving these joints. I'm coming to buy this shit like 3 or 4 times a week."

"I'mma see what I can do for you next time fool'. Let me holler at my people."

"Bet!" Dimp responded as he tossed the Macy's bag in his back seat. "Oh yeah, my man at the chop shop say he'll give you $25, 000 for that truck too.

"Aight bet. We on that tonight then." Colors responded. He really couldn't wait to get to the casino now. He had a $12, 500 cushion to play with. "Let me get up outta here though. I'll hit you up tonight."

"Aight. Tonight then." Dimp then pulled off thinking to himself, *I got this nigga right where I want him.*

* * * *

"I'm about to get up out of here." Jilla said to Camelle. "Dee gone come through in a minute. Give him these and put what he gives you in the closet.'" he said, pointing at the two duffel bags of money that were on the floor by the door.

Camelle looked up from the G.E.D. book that she was studying. "Where you about to go?" she asked.

"I gotta go take Dusty to rehab right quick. I'm gonna call you when we get done so we can go catch a movie or something."

Jilla knew he hadn't been spending too much time with Camelle due to the war with the *Break Bread* clique, him hustling, and the time he was spending with other chicks. Now that the war was officially won, more time was left to focus on her.

"Come lock the door." he said as he threw on his jacket.

Camelle got up off of the couch, walked over to the door where he was at, and grabbed his dick through his pants. "I want some of this when you come back." she said, kissing him on his cheek.

"I want some of that too." Jilla responded, slapping her on her ass.

Camelle then closed and locked the door, and went back to her studies. As she attempted to focus on her homework, the wetness that had formed in-between her legs was overwhelming. She stripped herself naked, popped in a porno movie, and pleasured herself with back to back orgasms. She was tired of doing that though. She felt that Jilla had been neglecting the pussy. She wanted to feel the dick inside of her on a consistent basis.

* * * *

Colors called up Dimp as he walked out of the casino. In ten hours, he had managed to lose the entire $50, 000 that Dimp had spent with him.

"Yeah." Dimp answered.

"What's happening fool?" Colors asked through the phone, as he pulled out of the casino parking lot, "Aye, I'm ready to take care of that other business while I got time. " he lied. Right about now, he had time to do anything to get that bread back.

"Man, I'm up at Chuck E Cheese right now. It's my lil daughter's birthday party going on. Give me about 3 hours and I'mma hit you back. "

"Bet. I'm on my way to the crib right now. I'm just gone lay back for a minute. As a matter of fact, you can just meet me there."

"I don't know where you live." Dimp replied.

Colors then gave him the directions to his apartment. "Just hit my phone when you on your way."

"Aight, I got you. As soon as the party over, I'mma get at you."

Colors figured he could pass the three in-between hours banging the Brazilian chick's back out some more. As soon as he hung up the phone, she reached over, pulled out his dick, and began sucking on it as he drove them to his apartment.

Just like he couldn't get enough of her, she couldn't get enough of him either. Once they reached his apartment, they engaged in round after round of more hot and steamy, nonstop, sex while he waited on Dimp's call.

* * * *

Camelle stood in the kitchen drying off the dishes she'd just washed. Singing along to the words of Keyshia Cole's *Love,* she was interrupted by the sound of the door buzzer. Getting up and walking to the intercom, she pressed the speak button. "Who is it?

"It's Dee. "

Camelle buzzed him in, then unlocked and opened the door, and waited for him to come up the stairs. When Dee made it to the door, she greeted him.

"Where you want me to put these at?" Dee asked, referring to the two backpacks with the bricks in them.

"Just put them right there on the side of the couch. That's what he left for you right there." she said, pointing to the two duffel bags full of money that Jilla had left for him.

"Aight bet." he said in-between breaths. "Y'all need to get an elevator or something in this motherfucker. A nigga fuck around and lose about five pounds just getting up the stairs."

"It's some bottled water in the refrigerator if you want one."

Just then Dee's cell phone rang. As he engaged in the conversation, that seemed to be another transaction, Camelle went back into the kitchen and proceeded to dry the dishes.

Damn, it seem like dat ass get bigger every time I see it Dee thought to himself as he was talking on the phone.

He suddenly felt his manhood begin to stiffen. "Aight fool, gimme a minute and I'mma ride down on you. " he said, ending the call. Making his way to the refrigerator, Dee purposely brushed up against Camelle's booty making sure she felt the stiffness that she'd caused him to develop.

She immediately stood on her tippy toes allowing him room to go by.

"My bad shorty." Dee said, looking deep into her eyes. Camelle didn't say anything. She just continued doing what she was doing, drying off the dishes.

"Aight I'm about to get on up out of here." Dee said, as he took a sip of the water and looked her up and down. He felt as if he was making Camelle uncomfortable and didn't want to overplay his hand. "Tell Jilla to hit me up when he ready again."

As Camelle led him to the door, his eyes were transfixed on how her ass jiggled. She was wearing a pair of grey cotton gym shorts with the word *Juicy* written across the back of them in black letters, and a grey cotton camisole top to match. The scent of her Victoria Secret body splash turned him on even more.

"See you Shorty."

"Bye Dee." she said, and hurriedly shut the door.

Leaning her back against it, and closing her eyes, she was glad that Dee was gone. There was no doubt about it that he had made her feel tingly sensations throughout her body that she knew only Jilla was supposed to.

* * * *

Red, Strawberry, and Passion were jamming to Beyoncé's latest C.D. on their way from serving one of Red's customers when her cell phone rang. When she heard Mary J. Blige's *Be Without You* ringtone' she knew it was Money.

"Heyy Boo-Boo." she answered.

"Damn Lil Mamma, turn that shit down." Money hollered into the phone.

Turning the volume down by the button on the steering wheel, Red then responded. "Okay baby, can you hear me now?"

"Yeah, now I can hear you."

"What's up with you?" she asked, blushing.

"Shit, thinking about you while we trying to get everything set up for the party tonight."

"What party you talking about? And who is we?"

"Me and a couple of my guys throwing a party at the Ice Bar tonight."

Money or Red hadn't formally introduced their friends to one another yet. All the time they'd been spending together had been one-on-one.

"That's why I wanted to call you. To see if you and your girls wanted to come through "

"Oh, so you want me to dance circles around you again?" Red joked.

"As long as I get to dance circles around you after the party's over." Money replied.

Red giggled and then heard him and some more people in the background laughing. "Who you with?" she questioned.

"Just me and a couple of my guys." Money replied.

"I guess we can step out tonight." Red said, as she looked back and forth between Strawberry and Passion. "I hope I don't bump into none of your little girlfriends."

Red threw that in the air just to see how Money would respond.

"You ain't gotta worry about that." Money shot back.

"I better not." Red responded. "So what time you want us to show up?"

"About 10:30ish is cool. How many people are you bringing with you?"

"Just me and my two girls."

"Aight. I'mma leave your name at the front door. Y'all ain't gotta wait in line. Just tell the door man who you is and y'all V.I.P. passes will be waiting there."

Just then Red's other line clicked. "Okay baby, let me get this other line. I'll see you tonight then."

"Aight, see you tonight beautiful."

After answering her other line and answering another sale, Red hung up her phone. Her phone started to ring again, immediately after she hung it up. This time the caller I.D. read UNAVAILABLE.

"Hello." she answered, as she turned off of 95th street onto Yates. What she heard made her pull over and park.

"Girl what's up." Passion asked from the back seat as she flicked the ash off of the blunt into the ashtray.

"Shh... Listen!" Red replied, activating her speaker phone so Passion and Strawberry could hear.

"Ha, ha, ha, ha. Wait till you see her. I guarantee she gone be shitting on every bitch up in that mufucka." Money had forgotten to hang up his cell phone. "Nigga and you should see her naked. She gotta flawless ass body from her head to her toes."

" Can she fuck though?" One of his homies asked.

" Can she fuck? She got the best pussy I ever had in my life. And that shit wet and tight too."

Red just listened as she felt her heart begin to beat faster and faster. Strawberry sat listening with her hand held over her mouth. And Passion sat scooted up in the back seat, holding on to the Blunt duck that was about to start burning her fingers.

"Can she suck a dick?" Another voice asked. Red figured that the other new voice had to be another one of his homeboys.

"Nigga that hoe sucked my dick so good, she made my toes get stuck. Curled up, for like three minutes. That bitch Super Head ain't got shit on her. She need to enter a dick sucking contest. Guaranteed she'll bring home that cash. " Money and all of his guys started busting up laughing.

Red felt her temperature begin to boil. One thing a woman never likes is for a man to reveal how she performs with the goodies. She actually thought that her and Money were building something special. From what she was hearing, it was evident that he felt otherwise.

"Man my nigga." he said, after they were done laughing

"I'm glad y'all did kill the boy Great. He left behind some grade A pussy. That freak bitch keep my dick hard."

Red damn near dropped the phone when she heard that. She immediately pressed the end button and powered her phone off. "I know that nigga didn't say what the fuck I thought he did!" Passion blurted out.

Red just sat there in total shock. Her complexion turned pale and tears began to roll down her face.

"Unh, unh. I'm calling Jilla and them right now."

Strawberry said, as she reached inside her purse to get her cell phone.

"Don't even trip girl." Red said, as she grabbed a McDonald's napkin out of her cup holder and wiped tears from her eyes. "I got these bitch ass niggaz. That's on Great. I got something for they hoe asses."

CHAPTER TWENTY-ONE

Dimp turned off of 159th street, headed to Colors' crib. D.E.A. agents had promised him that, instead of working for the entire two years after his release, he wouldn't have to put in anymore work if he successfully helped build a case against the *Bar None* crew. Pulling into the apartment complex, that was all that Dimp had on his mind.

He adjusted the three button Polo shirt that he was wearing, making sure that his wire was properly concealed and in a functioning position. As he dialed up Colors' number, all Dimp could think about was finally being free from the hooks that the Feds had in him.

"Yeah." Colors answered. He was inside of his apartment chain smoking cigarette after cigarette while sitting in the dark. The Brazilian chick was on the bed asleep, and the apartment reeked from the stench of sweaty sex and cigarette smoke.

"I'm outside fool." Dimp replied, as he scanned the parking

lot of the complex. "Bring me two of those thangs too. Ain't no use in me having to make two trips. I might as well kill two birds with one stone."

That's $70,000 Colors thought to himself. "Aight bet. Here I come right now."

He ended the call with Dimp and called up Dusty letting him know he had a two brick serve for him. Due to Colors not having any more work left, this was a time where living right next door to Dusty proved to be convenient. Dusty gave him the green light to come and get the two bricks.

After he left Dusty's apartment, Colors went into his garage to get the Cayenne truck. When he pulled around to the front of the complex, where Dimp was waiting, he parked, and then jumped out, making his way over to his Charger.

"What up fool?" Colors said, now sitting in the passenger seat of Dimp's car. He reached in-between his legs and pulled one of the bricks out the bag to show it to him.

"It's all good." Dimp responded, as he wiped the sweat off of his forehead with the back of his hand. "You ain't gotta keep showing me the cocaine every time I buy kilos from you. This is like the thirtieth time I done bought this shit from you within the last month and it's always the same thing. Crack cocaine."

Colors was so much in a hurry to get back to the casino, he hadn't even noticed how descriptive Dimp was with everything.

"Aight then, come on. Where the money at so I can go put that shit up and we can gone and get this shit over with. I got about three more people waiting on me." Colors lied, as he handed Dimp the coke. The script that he had initially given Dimp about not being in the game, and him working a construction job, had went out the window. Dimp had him right where he wanted him. "Damn nigga, you the sweatiest mufucka I done seen in my life."

Dimp had sweat pouring down his face. "Cause boy, you always making a mufucka feel like Mike Vick or some shit, the way you be rushing a nigga." Dimp said, as he grabbed the bag of money for Colors. "Here, that's forty-five thousand he continued, as he threw the bag into Colors' lap and lit up a cigarette.

Colors got out of the car and ran back to Dusty's apartment so that Dimp couldn't see where he was going. Little did he know, Dimp's eyes weren't the ones he had to worry about. As soon as he turned the corner, Dimp flicked his cigarette out the driver's side window. This was the signal to the awaiting agents that the drug deal was successful.

"All units it's a go!" an agent shouted into his radio. "Proceed with caution, proceed with caution."

As Colors came back around the corner, out of nowhere, he was surrounded by D.E.A. agents. "Hands in the air! Hands in the fuckin' air!" He heard continuously being shouted at him through the bullhorns. Red beam, after red beam, canvassed his body "On the ground and keep your hands where we can see them."

Colors instinctively looked around for an escape route, but they had him boxed in from every angle. There was nowhere to run. He laid on the ground and put his hands behind his head.

That bitch ass nigga Dimp, he thought to himself, *That bitch ass nigga Dimp*

* * * *

The line to get inside of the Ice Bar was wrapped around the corner. Red, Strawberry, and Passion walked pass the crowd and made their way to the front entrance. After giving Red's name to the doorman, the three of them were given green V.I.P. wristbands, and escorted to the section where Money, Mo, and Y.B. were.

The club was jammed pack from wall to wall. The girls even ran across a few of their customers and they greeted them as the bouncer led them through the crowd. All eyes seemed to be on the girls as they headed to V.I. P. Each one of them were dressed to impress and made up like Barbie dolls. Not a single lady in the building could tell them that they weren't shining, nor could one show them.

Money, Y.B., and Mo were sipping and tripping when Money noticed Red and the two other ladies being escorted up the stairs. He got up out of his seat and walked up to the railing so that he could get a better view. Y.B. and Mo followed suit. "Who is them right there?" Mo asked, as he noticed

Money and Red make eye contact.

"I know that ain't the mystery bitch that got your nose wide open is it?" Y.B. asked, now seeing for himself that she actually was as exclusive as Money had made her out to be.

"Yeah, that's her fine ass." Money replied, as he checked her out from head to toe. *God damn it oughta be a crime to be to be that damn fine* he thought to himself.

Red had on a blue House Of Dereon fitted dress, which showed off the curves of her body, and a pair of matching Prada heels. Her hair was done in a wrap style with flowing layers.

"Who them two bitches with her?" Mo asked, now eyeing Passion and Strawberry.

"Them the two bitches that was with her the day that I met her." Money replied, as he began to make his way toward the top of the stairs to meet them.

"I'm on the one right behind her." Mo said to Y.B., talking about Strawberry.

Strawberry stood 5 4" and was mixed with Korean and Black. Her chinky eyes, and high cheekbones, always made her short doo, hair style, look perfect. Not to mention the fact that the high waisted, True Religion jeans, and black see-through blouse that she wore, made her sexiness stand out even more. As she strutted in her Manolo Blahnik stilettos, Mo knew that he had to take her down.

"And I'm definitely on the other one." replied Y.B., as his eyes feasted on Passion.

Passion stood the tallest out of the three girls at 5'7'. By Y.B. being a light-skinned dude he had a thing for chocolate girls. Passion sported a pair of skinny jeans by Rock & Republic, and a sepia colored designer Chiffon blouse. Her hair was done in a bob, and her feet were adorned in a pair of Gucci heels. To best describe her, she resembled Keisha off of the movie, *Belly*.

Money returned to the table, all smiles, with the girls by his side. After introducing his guys to the girls, he and Red left so that he could show her off. Y.B. and Mo stayed in the V.I.P. section and entertained Passion and Strawberry.

* * * *

Jilla slowly bobbed his head to Fiends, *Murda On My Mind*, with a fifth of Hennessy in his left hand, a blunt in his right, and his pistol on his lap. His heart beat rapidly in anticipation of the moment that he'd been awaiting.

Yeah Great, I know you watching me right now, whether you're in heaven or hell. It's showtime, and I'm about to send these boys on a one-way trip, straight to where you at, so you can have your way with them. Jilla silently thought as his inner being spoke to Great. He then turned the liquor bottle up, took a swig, and handed it to Demon who was also in deep thought himself.

"I wonder why any mufucka in they right mind would cross us. They should know that the consequences ain't shit but death. This is what we do. Hustle, kill, and fuck bitches. The same shit that the niggaz that raised us did. If outsiders looking in can't figure that shit out, then they deserve to get just what these chumps about to get, put straight outta there misery."

Ugly, always being the quiet one, just sat in the back seat with his game face on. He had no thoughts. He just knew that it was time to put in that work. He was ready to let his guns do the talking.

Jilla's cell phone rang, breaking him out of his train of thought. Hearing the special ring from the blue phone, his adrenaline began to rush, figuring it was Red.

"Yeah."

"Baby where you at? "

Jilla pulled the phone away from his ear and looked at his caller I.D. to make sure he wasn't tripping. Instead of it being Red, it was Camelle calling him from their house phone. "I'm taking care of business baby. What's up, everything all good?"

"Colors is on the other line. He called collect and said he needs to talk to you. Some shit about it being an emergency."

"Click him in then." Jilla instructed her.

" Hello."

"What up fool? Where you at, calling collect and Shit?

"I'm knocked!!"

"Knocked? Where you at?"

"I'm at Cook County Jail. They just brought me here from the jail out by my crib."

"What they got you for? Never mind, never mind." Jilla caught himself and hurriedly said, remembering their means of conversing. As a rule, they never spoke too many words that could incriminate them while they were on their cell phones.

"You got a bond?"

"Yeah, my shit $50,000. Come get me outta here."

"Aight. Where your bread at?"

"They kicked in my door and took everything."

"What!!!" Jilla replied, still keeping his eyes focused on what they were before the call. "Dig, just chill for tonight and mufuckaz a be to get you first thing in the morning. "

"In the morning!! How come y'all don't come get me tonight?"

"You making me talk too much. First thing in the morning

mufuckaz a be to get you. On *Bar None.*"

"Say no more "

Jilla hung up the phone and told Demon and Ugly what was going on with Colors. Just as he finished telling them what was happening, his cell phone rang again.

****

Red got shown off to everybody at the party, danced a few rounds, and now was back seated in the V.I.P. section with Passion, Strawberry, Money, Y.B. and Mo. Bottles of Moet were being catered to their table all evening and dro' smoke filled the air, compliments of a few strings being pulled. The end of the party was nearing.

"Let's go have an orgy." Passion blurted out, as she got the cue from Red. She seductively twirled her straw around in her drink and licked her lips, ogling from Y.B., to Money, to Mo.

Mo couldn't believe his ears. His dick immediately began to get hard and Strawberry could feel it stiffening up while she sat on his lap. She took that as her cue. "Yeahh, that sounds like fun." she purred, rotating her ass against his hardness.

"They might not be able to handle that." Red cut in, looking Money in his eyes as if she were calling him out. "Those Blue Dolphins do got me horny. "

While they were smoking and drinking, Y.B. had handed out Ecstasy pills to everyone because all he had on his mind, from day one, was busting these girls down after the club. Pills had always been his way of getting women ready for whatever.

"Naw, I don't think *y'all* gone be ready." Y.B. said,

emphasizing the word y'all. Standing up, he then continued to get a deluxe suite on reserve at the Hyatt. "Let me go take care of something right quick and then we can gone and get up outta here. "

Red and Strawberry kept touching on, and whispering freaky shit in Money and Mo's ears while sitting on their laps.

Passion got up and made her way over to sit on Money's free leg so that he could enjoy her and Red in his ear at the same time. Whispering in his ear, she said, "I can't wait to see if you can make my pussy as wet as my girl said you did hers."

Money's dick felt like it was about to burst. Strawberry had her hand inside of Mo's pants, stroking him with her little fingers, while at the same time using her thumb to rub the pre-cum around the head of his dick.

"Man, where Y.B. go? I 'm ready to get up outta here." Mo said.

As soon as Young Jeezy's, *I'mma Tear Dat Pussy Up*, went off, the lights came on and Y.B.'s voice came blaring through the speakers. "Excuse me everybody. I'd like to thank each and every one of ya'll for coming through tonight in celebration of my nigga B-day." he said, while pointing over at Money, who was looking like a true player with Red and Passion both on his lap. "I hate to be the bearer of bad news, but it's time for us to bring it to an end. But before we go, I want to dedicate this last song to my three new friends, from me and my two niggaz." As soon as Y.B. finished his sentence, the lights dimmed, and Chris Browns, *Save The Last Dance* came on.

The girls all danced, and grinded on Money, Y.B., and MO one last time for the night. After the last dance was over with,

Red grabbed Money's manhood through his pants, and whispered in his ear again, "Take us where y'all gone take us baby. My pussy is hot as hell."

With that said, Money, Y.B., and Mo headed to the door with the girls following right behind. "Baby, I gotta go pee, Red whined. They waited at the front door while Red went to use the restroom. Passion and Strawberry continuously felt up Mo and Y.B. keeping them under their spell of seduction, "We about to leave out now." Red whispered into her phone from the stall she had ducked into.

She ended the call, checked herself out in the mirror, and pranced back out of the bathroom door.

As she made her way back to Money's side, she looked him up and down, smiling, while biting down on her bottom lip.

Even though he thought she was all smiles from thinking about the private after party that was about to go down, little did he know, she was really smiling at how Passion and Strawberry were doing their things. They had all three of the dudes wide open. Grabbing Money's hand, she led the party of six out the front door.

* * * *

"There they go right there." Demon said, sliding on a pair of black and grey Wilson baseball gloves.

Slim scanned through the crowd of people in the parking lot, making their way to the various vehicles, and started up the car. "Where they at? I don't see em."

"Right there. You don't see all them thirsty ass niggaz stalking?" Jilla replied, while pointing over Slim's shoulder.

"Oh, aight, aight. I see 'em"

* * * *

Money had instructed the girls to follow them to the hotel. The guys were in Y.B.'s Avalanche truck, and the girls were in Red's Durango. As they maneuvered through the lanes of the expressway, the guys were so driven by lust, that they didn't even detect the third car that was following them which was filled with killers.

Reaching the Hyatt, the guys and the girls parked their cars next to one another and proceeded to the hotel room. Once inside, the plan went into full effect.

* * * *

While they now waited in the parking lot for the last and final call, Jilla rolled another blunt of dro'. His patience was getting the best of him, and he could sense the eagerness in Demon, and Ugly as well. The 'dro served as something like a stabilizer and helped to sort of, ease their mind. But even with all of that said and done, they were ready to exact revenge and got tired of the waiting game.

Jilla's phone rang again. *Yes sirrr,* he thought to himself. Picking it up off of the seat next to him, he was disappointed to see that it was Camelle again.

"What's up baby?" he answered with a hint of agitation in his voice.

"Baby it's Dusty on the other line now. He say they got him too. "

"What!! Let me holler at him. "

Camelle put Jilla on hold for a second, then clicked back over connecting Dusty.

"What up Dusty? "

"I'm in the County. Them people kicked in my door, Colors ' too."

"Colors hit me a lil while ago. He ain't say shit about you getting knocked too though."

"That's because they got him first and then got me."

" How much is your bond?"

" Six-hundred thousand. Sixty to walk."

"Aight. I just need you to sit till the morning and we'll be to get y'all. You know what mufuckaz on right now."

Unlike Colors, Dusty knew where everybody was, and what they were on. By MO being Colors' cousin, they'd all agreed that it would be best that he wasn't let in on the murder game that was about to get laid down.

As soon as Jilla finished his sentence, the cell phone chimed, letting him know that he had a text message.

"Aight fool. Come get me in the morning. Don't have me sitting in this mufucka forever."

"I got you boy. There go that call right there. Let me go take care of this shit right quick."

"Bet. Be safe my nigga."

"Yep."

****

Everybody was inside of the Hotel room buck naked. In the

center of the room, was a king—sized bed where the girls had been getting down on each other for the last thirty minutes. The way they kissed and licked all over one another's bodies had Money and Mo itching to get their hands on them and join in on the fun. But every time they attempted to, the girls would tell them, "Not yet. Just enjoy the show first."

"I love these bitches." Mo said, after he took another swig of Moet.

After all three of the girls let the guys see them cum simultaneously, the shutters of each one of their bodies made them approach the bed. They couldn't take any more.

"Come and get this shit." Passion moaned, while laying on her back with her legs cocked in the air, opened wide. She rubbed her clit while looking at Y.B.

Strawberry was on her knees still sucking on Passion's breasts, as Mo slid up behind her. "Fuck this pussy from the back." she said to Mo, looking at him through the mirror she was facing as she licked around Passion's eraser sized nipple.

Red eased off of the bed as Money was approaching her. "I'll be right back for you Daddy. Mami gotta take a pee. Pick a hole till I get back, *any* hole." she seductively instructed, emphasizing the word any, as she looked over at the girls on the bed.

Money hopped onto the bed, and joined in on the party, as Red tip-toed toward the restroom on the balls of her feet. Before entering it, she dimmed the lights inside of the room, and turned the stereo system up a bit, so that Jamie Foxx's C.D. could work it's magic.

Grabbing her pocket book off of the table, without anyone noticing, she glanced over her shoulder at Passion and

Strawberry keeping the guys well occupied, and slipped inside of the restroom. She then sent Jilla the text message. *Room 408. Door unlocked. No guns.*

The whole purpose of getting Money, Y.B., and Mo naked was so that they could make sure that they didn't have any guns. Even though they were nowhere near the caliber of killers as the *Bar None* crew, they'd proven, when they offed Great and Lynn, that they would kill.

* * * *

Jilla, Demon, and Ugly crept up the stairwell until they reached the fourth floor. Gaining entrance to the Hotel through the front door was out of the question, due to the fact that they had on ski-masks and guns in their hands. Surprisingly, the side door was open and they didn't have to snatch any of the employees up to make them open it.

After finding room 408, Demon quietly turned the doorknob. Pulling the door open, enough for him to stick his head inside, he scanned the area. It was a full-time fuck fest going down. Him, Jilla, and Ugly eased their way inside, and shut, and locked the door.

Immediately, Jilla recognized Y.B. and his blood began to boil. Flicking the lights on, it was like he had pressed the pause button. The guys froze, knowing that they had just been caught slipping.

The girls immediately got up, began gathering up their clothing, and made their way over to the part of the room where Jilla and them were standing.

Jilla had the infra-red dot beamed right between the eyes of

Y.B., Demon and Ugly had their guns pointed at Mo and Money.

"Remember me mufucka?" Jilla asked, looking at Y.B. with the screwface.

The girls were now behind them, putting their clothes back on. Y.B., MO, and Money each had their hands in the air. "Damn, you goofies really got caught with ya'll pants down." Demon joked, as he moved in closer to Money.

"Let's hurry up and get this shit over with so we can get up out of here." Ugly said.

"Aight. So which one of ya'll mufuckaz pulled the trigger?" Jilla spat, not breaking eye contact with the red dot on the bridge of Y.B.'s nose for one second.

Neither Mo, Y.B., or Money said a word. Enraged by the sudden silence, Ugly smacked Mo upside his head with the butt of his gun, sending a chunk of meat, along with splatters of blood, flying across the room. "You heard what the fuck he asked. Who pulled the motherfuckin' trigger?"

"Man, I ain't have shit to do with that shit." Money pled.

Look at this scary mufucka, Red thought to herself, as her look shot daggers all through his body. Passion and Strawberry were now emptying out the money that they had in their pockets.

From Ugly pistol whipping him, Mo was left sprawled across the floor, holding his head, as blood gushed through his fingers. "Man, I don't know what y'all talking about." he whined, sounding like a little bitch.

All the time, Y.B. never said a word. Him and Jilla just held their stares.

"You know what the fuck I 'm talkin' about." Ugly said, as

he began stomping Mo out. "Which one of you bitch ass niggaz pulled the trigger on Great?"

"It wasn't me man. I promise it wasn't me man." Mo cried out.

"So, if it wasn't him," Jilla said, while taking the beam from in-between Y.B.'s eyes and beaming it down on Mo's chest, "or him," he continued, as he took the beam off of Mo, and beamed it on Money's throat, "that only leaves one person" he finished, now pointing the beam back on the bridge of Y.B.'s nose.

"I'm sorry man, but you seen how they got down on me that night. I had to get him back." Y.B. cried out, his silence broken. "I got cash man, don't even trip. You can have it all. Just don't kill us."

As good as that sounded to Jilla right then and there, seeing how he had to go bond out Colors and Dusty, he couldn't go for it. He even thought about getting the cash first, then killing them. He didn't have time for all of that though. He'd been waiting a long time to exact this revenge, so he had to roll with his adrenaline.

Like a well-rehearsed skit from a movie, Red turned the volume on the radio up sky high. FLACK! FLACK! FLACK! Jilla sent 3 shots flying into Y.B.'s face, leaving him slumped over with only half of it left.

BLACOW! BLACOW! BLACOW! BLACOW!

Ugly then sent four shots ripping golf sized holes through Mo's chest.

Just as Demon was about to put Money out of his misery, the radio cut off. Curious as to what had happened, everybody turned and looked toward the stereo system.

"I want this motherfucker. It's personal." Red calmly said, as she reached inside of her pocketbook. Pulling out a chrome plated .32 automatic, with a pearl handle, she walked up to Money, staring with vengeful eyes, pointing the gun at him. "I thought you had potential motherfucker. You turned out to be a bitch-made, sorry-ass nigga. How the fuck you gone try to outslick a can of oil." she continued, as she took her free hand and threw the three ecstasy pills that they'd given her, Passion, and Strawberry, earlier at the club, at him. "You or one of these dead motherfuckers." she went on, motioning her hand toward Y.B. and MO, "killed my man, and y'all thought y'all was gone just bust me and my girls down?" Glancing over at Passion, she gave her the cue to turn the radio back up. "Not in this lifetime bitch ass nigga. *Bar None* or nothing!" She then emptied every single round out of her clip into Money's body.

Demon then stepped up and hit him with three more shots to the dome, making sure that the job was completely done. After that, they wiped the entire hotel room down and got up out of there.

CHAPTER TWENTY-TWO

After leaving the hotel, they all met up in the parking lot of the projects. Exiting their cars, they headed towards the spot. Seeing how it was close to sunrise, quietness lurked through the air, and the sounds of birds chirping sung the tunes of Mother Nature.

Jilla felt good about getting Y.B. and them back for killing Great but, as they headed to the spot, his intuition had him feeling as if something just wasn't right.

As they headed up the stairs, Jilla and the *Bar None* crew, laughed at, and made fun of, the way they'd just did Y.B. and his boys.

"I still say we shoulda' took them chumps for they cash." demon blurted out.

"Hell yeah, especially since we gotta go bond Colors and Dusty out." Passion cosigned.

"Fuck that. That shit was personal." Jilla replied. as they made it up to the fourth floor.

The door to the spot had been kicked in. Noticing it, everyone stopped talking, something wasn't right.

"What the fuck!" Jilla whispered, looking over at everybody else.

He pointed his finger at the door, and everybody instantly pulled out their guns. Jilla quietly pushed the door open with his gun pointed out in front of him.

"Hit that light." he told Demon, nodding his head toward the switch.

Demon flicked the light switch on and the whole apartment was tossed up.

"Y'all wait right here." Ugly instructed Passion, Strawberry, and Red.

While they waited in the hallway, Jilla, Demon, and Ugly searched each room in the apartment to make sure that no one was still inside. After completing their search, the girls entered the apartment.

"Damn!! My mufuckin shit gone." Jilla said, coming out of the bedroom.

"What shit you talking about?" Demon asked.

"I had three hard ones, and one soft one, hid up under the bed in there." Jilla said, referring to four bricks he had stashed.

"I know ain't no mufucka played the stick-up game with us." Ugly said, as he picked up a cushion off of the floor and placing it back on the couch.

"Naw, it can't be that. Illa and Gadi ain't here. They woulda called. It had to be a raid or some shit." Red said.

Jilla and Demon were still busying themselves looking around the apartment for some sign as to what had really went down. Passion was getting a light for her cigarette off of the stove. Ugly and Red were sitting on the couch busting down blunt wraps.

"Here comes Uncle Petey." Strawberry announced, as she peeped out of the living room window. Through a slit in the curtain, she caught him entering the building.

Petey was Passion's Uncle, and also happened to be a crackhead. Everybody in the projects knew him and called him Uncle Petey. There wasn't one thing that went on in the projects that Uncle Petey didn't know about.

"Uncle Petey! Where Illa and Gadi at?" Passion asked, as she met him at the door, "What happened in here?"

Uncle Petey walked inside the spot, eyes wide as saucers, smelling like a garbage truck.

"The whole fourth district been up in here." he responded.

"I knew it was a raid." Red said, picking her gun up from beside her and placing it inside of her purse. Everybody began making their way towards the door.

"Fuck!!" Jilla hollered. He then walked to the window and took a quick peek out of it.

"Illa got into it with one of them Hispanic boys over there around the corner, and got to shooting at him. Just so happen, a detective car was coming around the corner and caught him dead in the act. Illa took off running and ran straight here." Uncle Petey was talking fast, rocking side to side like he had to use the restroom. "Them people seen him and run right up in here behind him. Ms. Powell, downstairs, said it took three kicks to knock down the door. All I know is I seen 'em taking Illa and Gadi up outta here in handcuffs, and they came up out of here with two big ole paper bags full of something."

"Damn, luckily them niggaz juveniles, so they should be all

good. " Ugly said, Jilla then reached inside his pocket and pulled out a roll of money. "I want you to go down to the police station and see if you can get 'em out. If you can't, just find out what's up with them and hit me up on my horn to let me know." Jilla peeled off two $50 bills and gave them to Uncle Petey.

"Oh yeah, let me give you the alias names they should be under too."

Jilla then picked an empty blunt box up off of the floor and tore a piece off. After writing the alias on it, he handed it to Uncle Petey as well.

"Aight nephew." Uncle Petey replied, showing the last two rotten teeth in his mouth, with a smirk. "You ain't got nothing else for me?" he slid in, referring to some crack.

"Come on. You asking for too much now." Passion said, as she grabbed him by his arm and led him towards the door.

"Yeah, let's get up out of here before them people reroute and all of us be in somebody's jail cell." Demon said.

They all left and made their way to the parking lot where the guys piled in Jilla's truck, and the girls piled in Red's. They each agreed to head home and get a couple hours of sleep before the morning, when it would be time to go bond Colors and Dusty out.

* * * *

The next morning, Jilla counted out $40, 000 and began to make his way to the front door of his apartment. All together they had to come up with $110,000 to cover Dusty and Colors' bonds. Twenty from Demon, Twenty from Ugly, twenty from Red, five from Passion, and five from Strawberry. That, on top of Jilla's forty, put them where they needed to be.

"Where you going this early?" Jilla heard. as he threw the strap of the gym bag over his shoulder.

Camelle rubbed her left eye with her knuckle, as she sat up in the bed, resting on her elbow.

"I'm about to go round up the rest of this money, so we can bond Dusty and Colors out, then I gotta go see what's up with Illa and Gadi."

"You always gotta go do some shit that got to do with your friends. You ain't never got time for me."

Here we go, Jilla thought to himself.

"Look, as soon as I get through taking care of this shit, I'mma call you, and tell you to get ready so we can go wherever you want."

"Whatever Jilla." she said. Rolling her eyes, and then smacking her lips, Camelle then got out of the bed and headed to the shower.

Seeing her ass jiggle, Jilla realized how he actually had been neglecting the pussy.

"For real. As soon as I get done with this, I promise, it's you and me. Wherever you want to go."

"How long is that going to take? "

"Let's see. It's eleven now, I should be through with everything by about seven tonight."

"Whatever, I guess I'mma go to the mall and get me something to wear for tonight. I need some money."

Jilla sat the bag down by the door, ran back to his safe, and got a couple of racks out for her. *Damn, my money starting to look funny* he thought to himself.

"I'm leaving some money on the dresser for you. Make sure you get something sexy to wear for Daddy too. "

Jilla then grabbed the bag again and headed out the door. As soon as she heard the door shut and lock, Camelle was out of the bathroom, calling her friend so she wouldn't have to shop alone.

* * * *

Sitting on 26th and California, Jilla and Demon puffed on a blunt as they waited for Colors and Dusty to be released. Cook County Sheriff cars, detective cars, and Chicago Police Department cars consistently riding pass, had both of them paranoid and on full alert.

"There they go right there, " Jilla said, sitting up in his seat and starting up the van,

After getting shot, Dusty traded in his Impala for a custom-made conversion van which he could operate from the steering wheel. He also had one of the seats in the back taken out so that his wheelchair could sit in its place.

"What type of bird don't fly?" Demon joked, as they pulled off.

Jilla started laughing as he looked at his two, fresh out of jail, homeboys through the rear-view mirror. While Dusty had a look of relief on his face, he noticed that Colors didn't look like his normal self.

I know he ain't letting one night in jail shake him up, Jilla thought to himself. He'd known Colors for way too long and could tell that something was worrying him.

"What up fool?" How the fuck y'all get knocked?" Jilla

asked.

"I don't know. All I know is them bitches came out of nowhere, kicking in my door. When they took me to the car, I seen Colors' shit kicked in too." Dusty said, as he grabbed the blunt from Demon.

Colors just sat in his seat like he was in some kind of trance. All that he could think about was Dimp. He didn't even notice Jilla's eyes beaming down on him. All Colors could think about was how everything that was going on at the moment, was all his fault.

"What up with you boy? Why you so quiet and shit?" Demon asked Colors.

Fool must 've read my mind, Jilla thought to himself. He drove, not saying a word, but still studying Colors through the rear-view mirror.

"Damn, my bad." Colors said, broken out of his train of thought. "I'm just sitting here trying to figure out who the fuck sent them people at us like that. That was a big hit we took, and that shit don't carry no little ass time either."

"I know fool, cause you and the lil dude both in the rear with the whole squad." Jilla said, pointing his eyes from Colors to Dusty, through the rear-view mirror.

"Man, fuck what they in the rear. The shit gone get right back one way or the other. If we don't hustle up on it, then we just gone take something. Who got them loose lips is the issue at hand?" Demon spat.

"Hell yeah. " Dusty added in.

"Plus lil' Illa and Gadi got knocked last night too."
said Jilla.

"Get outta here. How they get knocked?" Colors asked.

"Illa got in a shoot-out with them lil' Spanish boys and ran right to the spot. Uncle Petey say them people ran right in there behind him."

"Whaaatt?" Colors replied.

"I took another loss with that shit too. I been getting hit upside the head all around the board lately." Jilla said, "Did Uncle Petey ever call you to let you know what was up with them lil' niggaz?" Demon asked.

"Yeah. He say they ain't got no bonds, and they charged them as adults."

"Oooh wee, Dusty said.

"They solid though. They ain't gone play the telling game." Demon shot back.

Colors' mind was working overtime, wondering if Dimp had something to do with the little homies getting locked up too. Even though Uncle Petey said the shoot-out and foot chase had led them to the spot, Dimp was the prime suspect on everything right now as far as he was concerned. As bad as he wanted to tell the guys about him right now, he couldn't. Deep down inside, he felt that all types of drama was about to unfold, all because of him fucking with Dimp.

"What's up with everybody else?" Dusty asked.

"They all good. Everybody supposed to be meeting up over here now." Jilla said, as he turned onto Red's block. "I can't fuck with y'all for too long though, I gotta make a few moves. Plus, I gotta spend some time with Camelle tonight. "

"What the plate looking like? I'm ready, plus Ugly say he dumping the last of his shit and meeting us over here." Demon said to Jilla, letting him know that they were ready to re-up. "Y'all say ya'll got court in the morning right?" Jilla asked Colors and Dusty.

"Yeah, we got court at ten-thirty and Mitch say he want us at his office at eight sharp." Colors responded.

Mitch was a beast in the court room. He was known for beating cases. Not only was he a well-connected attorney, but he knew his law as well. Any hustler in the city of Chicago knew that Mitch was the man to represent you on any drug or gun charge. You had to have that grown man money to hire him though. He knew that, he was what was happening.

"Aight bet. I'mma hit Dee up and let him know that I'll be over to holler at him tomorrow. The price of tea in China gone have to rise though. My order about to be half of what it usually be."

After pulling into Red's apartment complex, they exited the van and headed to her apartment to celebrate Colors and Dusty's release. Jilla had a million things going through his head. A lot of tightening up had to get done.

* * * *

"Will that be for here or to go?" The cashier asked Dee, after taking his order.

"For here. "

After getting the food, he headed over to the table.

Sitting the tray down, his cell phone began ringing.

"Yeah." he answered.

"What up fool?"

"Shit, what up with you? Long time no hear."

"I know, I know. Shit been going a lil fucked up on my end of town lately. It's all good though. It ain't no storm a nigga can't weather. I'm trying to see you tomorrow though. What your life like?"

"It's all good. You still throwing the same pitches?"

"Naw, I'm working on my changeup. Only focusing on half of the plate." Jilla said, using code to let Dee know that he only wanted to purchase half the amount of bricks that he usually did.

Dee already knew what had gone down with Colors and Dusty and he figured that they'd brought the heat on themselves from something stupid that they'd done. He wanted so badly to tell Jilla *I told you*, but decided against it. Knowing how much of a hot head he was when somebody tried to tell him something, he just let Jilla do him. If he wanted to keep dropping bond money, and paying lawyer fees, that was on him. He was just going to make as much money off of Jilla as he could.

"I hear you. Each strike you throw gotta be a little higher in the zone though." Dee told Jilla, letting him know that the prices were going to be higher than usual.

"What you mean? How much higher? "

"Like a stack. My people got down on me like that, so 1 gotta get down like that too. That's the only way I get to make a little something. It should only be like this this one time though."

Everything seemed to be going wrong for Jilla right about now. His money was getting low, his guys had been getting knocked, and he'd been taking all kinds of losses. Now Dee was talking this raising the price's bullshit. If he could, he would've just stopped fucking with Dee all together. However, he couldn't though, because he didn't have another connect to replace him with.

"Aight man." Jilla said disappointingly. "I'mma hit you up when I'm ready tomorrow."

"Aight. I'mma holler at you tomorrow then."

Dee ended the call, sat his phone down on the table, and picked up his chicken wing. Taking a bite of it, he looked across the table with a smirk on his face.

"Now, back to you little Miss Beautiful."

Camelle just blushed, as she chewed on her Caesar Salad. As soon as Jilla had left the apartment, she immediately called Dee and told him to meet her at Orland Square Mall. Not only had Dee been spending the quality time with her that Jilla hadn't, he also handled the shopping tab that she ran up every time they met at the mall.

"Whatever." she responded dabbing around her mouth with a napkin. "Was that Jilla?"

"Yeah, that was your man."

"What he say?"

"He just said he was going to be to holler at me tomorrow. I hope you be wearing something out of there when I get there." Dee said, pointing at the Victoria's Secret bag that was sitting on the floor next to the table.

Jilla and Dee no longer met face to face when they took care of business too much. He'd been so caught up in the streets that he'd just have Dee drop the work off to Camelle and she'd make the transaction.

"I gotta go then. That means he'll be on his way home to get me in a few. Thank you for the lunch and clothes." Camelle said, holding up the two arm fulls of shopping bags.

"Anything for you, my best kept secret."

Camelle's cell phone began to ring. Sitting the bags back down, she pulled the phone out of her purse. Noticing Jilla's number on the caller I.D., she held her index finger to her lips signaling for Dee to be quiet as she answered.

"Hello."

"What up? Where you at? "

" Getting ready to leave the mall."

"Aight, which one you at?"

"Lincoln Mall." she lied.

"Bet, I'mma be ready in a couple of hours, so make sure you be ready when I get there. "

"Okay baby."

"Aight."

"Love you. "

"Now you love me huh? Miss Bi-Polar."

"Whatever boy."

"Aight, in a couple."

"Okay, bye-bye."

Camelle ended the call and placed her phone back inside of her purse. Dee then walked her back to her car. After saying their goodbyes, she headed home.

Camelle knew she was playing with fire. Dee gave her

something that Jilla didn't. He spent quality time with her. The same quality time that would come to be the beginning of her ending.

CHAPTER TWENTY-THREE

The ringing of Jilla's cell phone woke him up out of the comatose like sleep that he was in. He was supposed to had met the guys at Mitch's office but, due to how late him and Camelle had stayed out, he hadn't waken up in time.

"Where you at?" Demon shouted loudly into Jilla's ear.

"What time is it?" Jilla whispered, as he glanced over at Camelle who laid asleep next to him. "It's ten o'clock fool."

"Damn, I was knocked out."

Camelle had worn him out pretty good after they had come back from the comedy club. She had even busted out a few sex tricks on him that he'd never seen her do before. He figured it must have been the Pina Coladas she had drank, mixed with the pornos he had always brought home.

"We about to be pulling up to the court building in a couple of minutes. That fool Mitch say he need to holler at you too."

"Man, by the time I throw on some clothes and shit, and get down there, court will be over. Just call me when ya'll get outta there. I'm about to get this bread together so we can get back right."

"Aight, we should be in and out of this bitch anyway. They ain't about to do shit but give them a continuance."

"Bet. Hit me back when y'all leave then. Luv my nigga."

"Luv."

After Jilla sat his phone back down, he looked over at Camelle again. Peeping up under the cover, her nakedness made him horny all over again. His dick began to stiffen up, and he reached his hand up under the cover until his fingers founds their way in-between her legs. Rubbing up and down her slit made Camelle begin to stir out of her sleep with a slight moan. As she moaned, she became wetter and wetter. Arching her back, she urged his fingers to proceed. After getting her all worked and lubed up, he climbed on top of her and replaced his fingers with his manhood. Instead of giving it to her fast and hard, like he had the night before, he pleased her with long, deep, and slow strokes. She closed her eyes, and bit down on her bottom lip, enjoying every single inch of him.

The wetness of Camelle's pussy caused Jilla to cum hard. After he came, Jilla rolled over on his back and enjoyed the sensations that were running through his body, while at the same time, trying to catch his breath. Camelle then got on top of him and slid his dick right back into her pussy. She wasn't going to let him go limp without her cumming one more time.

Riding him, reverse cowgirl style, Camelle's ass bounced up and down. Jilla took his hands and spread her ass cheeks apart so that he could get deeper inside of her.

"Oooh daddy. I 'm about to cum." she purred, as she increased the speed of her bounce.

As her hands tightened the grip on his legs, she bounced up and down on Jilla wildly, balancing herself on the balls of her feet.

"Ooh Jilla, shit."

Just as she was about to cum, Jilla's phone rang.

Bling, Bling, Bling.

The sound of it messed her whole groove up. Jilla reached over to answer the phone.

"Shit!!" Camelle pouted, as she climbed off of him. Due to her concentration being broken, she didn't even get to get her nut off.

As Jilla answered the call, Camelle sat straight up against the headboard of the bed, with her arms folded across her chest, and poked out her bottom lip.

"What up?"

"The Feds just snatched Colors and Dusty up out of the court room."

"What!" Jilla shouted, sitting up in the bed.

"Me and Ugly out in the hallway waiting on their court to be over with, and I'm on the phone with this freak bitch talking dirty in her ear. Ugly then taps me on my arm and point at three U.S. Marshals walking Colors and Dusty up outta there with cuffs on. " Demon informed him.

"How you know it was the Marshalls?"

"Nigga, them chumps had big shiny ass gold badges. Plus, Mitch told me. He say the Feds is out his league cause he ain't federally licensed. He say he gone put us in the car with one of his lawyer buddies that's cold with the Fed law though."

"Bet, that's what's up. Where ya'll at now?"

"We riding down California, getting ready to jump on the

E-Way."

"Man, this shit is crazy. Mufuckaz can't win for losing. We need to meet up though. Hit the girls up and tell them we at Bensley Park in thirty minutes."

Hanging up the phone, Jilla got up out of the bed and went into the bathroom to take a shower. After he was done, he walked back into the bedroom with a towel wrapped around his waist.

Camelle still sat up in the bed with her back against the headboard. She now had two pillows propped up behind her back as she watched a movie on the Lifetime channel. As Jilla grabbed a pair of boxers out of the dresser drawer, she couldn't help but notice, through the mirror, him drop the bath towel to the floor. As she watched him, her pussy began to jump, seeing him naked, dick swinging.

"Oh, so you just gone up and leave me again just like that? Without even finishing what you started?"

"Camelle, not right now. Some real important shit just came up that I gotta go tend to immediately."

"You need to be tending to your woman's needs immediately Jilla. That's what you need to be tending to."

Jilla didn't even respond to her. He finished getting dressed and headed out the door. Camelle knew that it really was some important shit going on. She might not have known all the details, but she did hear the word Feds. She knew that that had to mean trouble. Instead of being understanding, she took the moment as an opportunity to pick a fight with Jilla so that she could justify, in her own little mind, what she was about to do.

* * * *

Bling, Bling, Bling... Bling, Bling, Bling...
"Hello."

"Jarian." Jilla's mother hollered through the phone addressing him by his government name. "What the hell you done went and gotten yourself into?"

"What you talking about Ma? I ain't did nothing."

"Boy, about six police cars just left my house looking for you. They talking about they got a warrant out for your arrest."

" For what?"

"Boy, I don't know. All they told me is you know what's going on."

"What, was they regular police officers?"

"They all had on plain clothes and two of them had on blue jackets with the letters D.E.A. wrote on the back."

Jilla just remained silent. Things had gotten real real hot all of a sudden. He knew that, at this point, it had to be all about survival of the fittest. Somebody was attracting the heat though. When he found out who it was, the ultimate punishment would be handed out.

"Boy do you hear me?" His mom shouted through the phone.

"What you done went and did?

"I ain't did nothing."

"Well they left their card here and told me to tell you to call them if I hear from you. If you ain't did nothing then you need to turn yourself in and see what they want. "

"Yeaahhh?" Jilla responded, knowing that the catcher came before the hanger. The day that he turned himself in to any type of police would never come. "Aight, I'mma come over there and get the card from you so I can call them. The battery on my phone about to die so it's going to hang-up. I'll be over there."

Jilla then slammed his phone down in his passenger seat. He had to figure out how to get out of this jam.

* * * *

"Dunston, upper seven, you got a visit. "

Colors was in the dayroom gambling on the spade table when he heard his name get called over the intercom. After he finished playing his hand out, he went to his room, got his visiting outfit from under his mattress, and changed into it. Due to their being no iron inside the jail he was being held at, the only way to get creases was to fold his clothes neatly, then put them under your mattress, and sleep on them.

"A Nickel Slick." Colors yelled from the doorway of his cell.

"What up?"

"Check it out right quick fool."

Nickel Slick got up from the table in front of the T.V. in the dayroom, and jogged up the stairs to Colors' cell.

"What up Colors? It's some bad ass bitches on Maury nigga. What the fuck you want?"

"I'm about to go on a visit. Hold these til I get back." Colors reached up under his pillow and grabbed two homemade knives that looked like ice picks.

"Damn nigga, now I got four shanks on me." Nickel Slick said, lifting his uniform shirt up. "A, I know you finna go see one of them bitches too. Tell her to hook me up with one of her friends."

"I got you fool. I don't even know who it is though. Motherfuckers on some pop up, surprise shit, trying to catch a nigga up. Whoever it is though, I'mma try to put something together for you for next week."

"Bet my nigga."

Nickel Slick went back to finish looking at Maury, and Colors made his way to the corridor to check out for his visit. After patting him down, the C.O. radioed the door open so Colors could proceed to the visiting room.

Once inside, the C.O. instructed Colors to make a right instead of a left. "That way. Room three. You have an attorney, not personal visit."

Must be my lawyer, Colors thought to himself. He went into room three and took a seat.

As Colors sat patiently, he wondered what type of news his lawyer had for him. Good news was all that he wanted to hear.

Hearing the doorknob move, he turned around to greet his attorney. The sight he saw, disappointingly, was not what he had expected. Two white men, that he'd never seen before, entered the room. The badges clamped to their belts had the letters D. E. A. sprawled across the top of them in big, blue, shiny, letters. In each of their hands were file folders that had classified written on the front of them.

"Mr. NaRico Dunston." the first agent said. "I'm agent Sanders, and this is my partner, agent White." he continued, while extending his hand to Colors for a handshake. Colors just stared at his hand like it had poison on it, not saying a word. "Okay, I'm not for all the small talk either." agent Sanders continued, now pulling out a chair from the opposite side of the desk that Colors was seated at. "You're part of an ongoing investigation that we've been working on, and you're facing serious charges which carry up to life in prison." He then opened up one of the file folders and turned it around on the desk so that Colors could see it. "Do you recognize any of these individuals?"

He had pictures of everybody; Jilla, Demon, Ugly, Dusty, Red, Passion, and Strawberry. It was even pictures of Slim, Great, Luke, and Rello with the word *deceased* stamped across each of their faces.

"Naw, I don't know none of them." Colors said, as he pushed the pictures away from him, and back towards the agent.

Sanders then looked over at agent White, giving him a smirk.

Agent White then walked over to the table and picked up another file. Opening it up, he removed another set of photos. "Well how do you explain this if you don't know any of them?" he asked, throwing the set of pictures down on the desk in front of Colors.

This time, the photos showed all of them, together, at different points of times. Coming from clubs, walking out of malls, leaving liquor stores, etc. "How could you not know people who we have you on camera socializing with? Do you socialize with people without knowing them all the time?"

"Man, I need to talk to my lawyer. I ain't got shit else to say."

"You can make this hard on yourself if you want to. Either you help us out, or you can get ready to spend the next thirty years to life behind bars."

Colors just got up out of his seat and opened the visiting room door to leave. "I'm done. Send me back up to my unit." he said to the C. O. who was monitoring the door.

After Colors left, they called Dusty down from his unit and got the same results. None!!!

CHAPTER TWENTY-FOUR

A month had passed, the walls seemed as if they were closing in on the *Bar None* crew. The Feds, and local authorities, were flooding the entire East-Side, making it hot on every set. The entire *Bar None* crew sold their cars and jumped in rentals, switching up every week.

Their pictures were being posted up almost everywhere, with the words WANTED written over the top of them. This made it difficult for them to move around the city in the daytime. Especially with the $10,000 reward that was offered for information leading to their capture. Everyone was now staying in separate motels scattered throughout the city.

"Damn, this nigga Dee ain't been answering his phone all motherfuckin' day." Jilla said, as they all sat in Slim's motel room.

"Man I keep telling you we need to stick that scarey ass nigga up. I don 't know why you keep harboring that chump." Demon replied.

"Hell yeah fool. Plus, that nigga keep taxing the shit out of us." Ugly added in.

"Aight, if we stick him, who we gone get our work from?" Jilla shot back.

"Niggaz just gone have to find another connect." Demon retorted.

"That chump ain't the only motherfucker in the city with work." Ugly added again.

"Naaah, anybody but him." Jilla said, shaking his head.

"He been loyal to us from day one."

"That nigga ain't *Bar None*. Fuck him!" Demon said.

"The cash gettin' low Jilla, we need a stang. The whole crew feeling this on the run shit. Then this hoe ass nigga on some taxing shit." Ugly threw in.

"Don't trip, we'll find a stang. We can hit the club and get on a niggaz bumper. Not Dee though, we need him."

* * * *

"Where y'all at?" Red asked Demon.

"We up at Ugly's room waiting on this nigga Dee to call back so we can get back right."

"What Jilla doing?"

"He calling Camelle to see if Dee done left a message for him."

"I bet she don't answer."

"Why you say that?"

"Just wait a second and see."

Demon nonchalantly cut his eyes over at Jilla and watched him hit the end button on his phone aggravatingly. "Man, what you on? You think you a psychic or some shit?" he asked Red.

"Naw. Me, Passion, and Strawberry sitting here looking at her and Dee all hugged up and shit. They coming out of the movie theater."

Demon almost choked on the swig of Heineken that he'd just taken." Wh... what you just say?"

"Give Jilla the phone!" Red shouted.

"Naw, fuck that. I'm putting my shit on speaker phone."

Demon activated the speaker phone on his cell and threw it on the bed that Jilla and Ugly were sitting on, as they were recounting the money.

"Jilla!" Red Shouted.

"What up girl?" Where you at?"

"Sitting right here watching your little bitch all hugged up with this nigga Dee."

Jilla stopped counting the money and froze. Ugly looked up as well, knowing he hadn't heard what he thought he did.

"Who you talking about." Jilla asked, breaking the silence that had grabbed ahold of the motel room.

"Camelle. And we about to get out and beat her little ass." Passion said.

Her and Strawberry began pinning their hair up in ponytails, as Red sat her phone down in the cup holder so she could pin her hair up as well.

"And if this nigga Dee try to play captain save a hoe, I'mma pop his feminine ass." Red said.

Jilla's heart was crushed. Refusing to show it, he maintained his composure. "Naw, naw don't do shit. Just get a picture of them on your cell phone for me and send it to mines. Y'all forgot y'all got warrants? We finna cash in again, don't even trip."

* * * *

The next morning, Jilla left his motel room with Lashonna. She was a light-skinned, aspiring model, that he had met one day when he was at the citywide all-star basketball game.

Lashonna was mixed with white and Puerto Rican. The light freckles that were on both sides of her face, enhanced her skin tone and face structure, giving her a unique type of beauty. That, along with her hourglass shape, and curly hair, made her by far, the finest thing at the game. After a few dates and nights of after hour fun, she became one of the many dime pieces that he'd count on when he needed them.

As they headed downtown, Jilla coached her on what she needed to ask, and say, to Colors and Dusty. Due to the Feds having a search warrant out for the arrest of the remaining members of the *Bar None* crew, none of them had spoken to Dusty or Colors since they'd gotten snatched up out of court. The average individual would have been upset or offended. But Colors and Dusty both knew why they hadn't heard from them. It would have been like walking into a death trap.

After they arrived at the federal building, Jilla parked. Lashonna got out of the car and headed for the front entrance. Once she entered, Jilla reclined back the driver's seat, and sparked up a blunt. He had a lot on his mind.

Breaking him out of the zone that Tupac's, *Hail Mary*, had him in, Jilla's phone rang. The number with the 312-area code was unfamiliar. Because of that, he answered it with his best impression of a woman's voice.

"Hellooo."

"Hello, may I speak to Jilla?" A heavy accented male voice asked from the other end of the phone.

Not catching on to who it was, Jilla continued to disguise his voice. "May I ask who's speaking?"

"I'm sorry. Do I have the right number? This is Flaco and I'm looking for Jilla."

Able to match the voice with the name, Jilla spoke with his normal voice. "Flaco? This you? Where you been man?"

"Whoa, whoa, whoa, mi amigo. I'm sure we have a lot of catching up to do. How about tonight around eleven. I'll give you a call and we'll go have a nice time. Then we can talk."

"Sounds like a plan to me Flaco. I'll be waiting on your call."

Flipping his phone shut, and looking up, Jilla spotted Lashonna coming out of the building looking like the young model she was. As he started the car up, she opened the passenger side door, and got back into the car.

"What dey say?" he asked as he pulled out of the parking space.

"Okay, first I called Colors out. He said they went to court the other day and they got charged with conspiracy, felon in possession of a firearm, and possession of a controlled substance. He said he didn't want to do too much talkin' in the visiting room but to tell y'all to *lay low* because they're looking for y'all too. He said when he finds out more, he'll find a way to send you a message so you can send me back to holler at him."

"And Dusty?"

"He said the Feds tried to come and squeeze him for some information but under the *Real Nigga Act,* wasn't shit shaking. He said he got those same charges too and they got some confidential informants who he's waiting to get the names of. He said that there definitely are some motherfukers out there talking and that it definitely was a set up. Oh yeah, he said he's been getting rehabbed while he's been in there and he got a little bit of feeling on his left leg."

"Dat's good shit." Jilla replied, referring to Dusty beginning to regain felling in his leg.

After they ate lunch at Red Lobster, he dropped Lashonna off at her apartment and gave her $500 for taking care of the business.

Jilla then called the rest of the crew, letting them know one by one, the good news about hearing from Flaco. He also informed them on the information that Colors and Dusty had sent through Lashonna. Hanging the phone up, his thoughts drifted to Camelle. He had to confront her.

* * * *

Sliding in the back door of the building Camelle and him lived in, Jilla crept his way up the back stairs. After entering his condo, he shut and locked the door to the apartment. Walking into the bedroom, he found Camelle laid in the bed asleep.

Look at dis slut ass bitch, he thought. to himself. *Hoe been out fuckin' all night, now she sleep at two o'clock in da muthafuckin' afternoon.*

"Bitch get yo' ass up!" He yelled pointing the 9-millimeter at her head.

Camelle jumped up out of her sleep from the loudness of Jilla's voice. Opening her eyes, all she saw was the barrel of the gun he was holding, aimed straight at her face. "Boy stop playing with that damn gun. What's wrong with you? You been drinking?"

"Do I look the fuck like I'm drunk hoe?" Jilla shouted as he charged toward where she was in the bed.

Drawing his free hand back to the other side of his face, so that his palm was facing his cheek, he back slapped her in one sweeping motion with all of his might.

SMACK!

Camelle fell off of the bed onto the floor. Holding her face she cried, "Jilla, what's wrong with you?"

Jilla then slammed the butt of his gun on her head. "Bitch you don' t know what the fucks wrong with me?"

As blood ran down the side of Camelle's face onto the hardwood floor of their bedroom, she held her face in her hands attempting to cover up. "Oh God, please help me." she sobbed in-between whimpers.

Reaching up under the long blue T-shirt that he was wearing, Jilla unsnapped his phone from the clip that was attached to his belt. Flipping it open, he scrolled to the pictures of her and Dee, that Red had taken and sent to his phone, and bent down holding the phone up to Camelle's face.

"Your slut ass crossed me for dis bitch ass nigga here?" Camelle's heart felt like it had stopped beating. She opened her mouth to talk but no words came out. She was stuck.

CRACK! Jilla hit her with a left hook that shattered her

entire jawbone. After constantly kicking and stomping her, he stopped; unzipped his jeans, and pissed all over her from her face to her feet. Camelle laid there in a puddle of piss and blood crying.

Breathing hard, with foam forming in the crevices of his mouth Jilla cocked back the hammer of his Ruger. "Bitch you love dat nigga?" he growled bending down and thrusting his heater into her throat.

"No...oo..o., " she mustard out while gagging.

"You gone die for dat nigga?" Jilla shouted now sweating profusely himself.

"Nooo..."

"Hoe you only got one way to save yo' life. Where dat nigga keep all his shit at?"

Dee had taken Camelle to his safe house on a few occasions due to people calling and placing orders with him while they were together. She knew that Jilla was a killer and saw the murder in his eyes so deciding between Dee's wealth and her life wasn't a hard decision for her to make.

"At his grandmother's house in her basement, Jilla I'm sorry."

Jilla stood back up and got to pacing back and forth inside the bedroom thinking about his next move. Gripping his gun with animal strength, he went back over to where Camelle was balled up laying on the floor. Grabbing a fist full of her hair and turning her face towards his, she looked at him with pleading eyes. Her face was covered with blood, and sweat, and thick globs of mucus were running from her nose. "Hoe the first time you cross me, it's yo' fault, the second time you cross me, it's mine for lettin' you stay alive to do it. Ain't gone be no second time wit' me."

BAAK! BAAK! BAAK!

Jilla let several shots off into the back of her head. "*Bar None* bitch." he said as he spat on her. He then bolted for the door.

CHAPTER TWENTY-FIVE

Later that night Jilla entered a Mexican bar on the west side, down the street from Humboldt Park. Latin music hummed through the speakers as a few drunken couples did the Zapateado. As he gazed around in search of Flaco, thick smoke consumed the room making it difficult to spot him.

"Hola, Senor Flaco te esta esperando alla." a Mexican Lady greeted Jilla.

Not understanding a bit of Spanish, he really didn't know what she had just said to him. Out of the entire sentence he only understood one word, Flaco. Hearing that name was all that he needed to oblige to the hand gesture she'd given him to follow her.

Seated over in a corner was Flaco puffing on his signature Cuban Cigar. "I take another shot of Brandy and a bottled water for my friend here." he said to the waitress.

"Nah, make dat a double shot of Hennessy." Jilla cut in.

After giving the waitress a head nod of assent, she left to place the order and Flaco looked over at Jilla. "Drinking now my young friend?" he questioned inquisitively.

"Not really." Jilla lied. "I just got a few things on my mind tonight, plus I'm hoping today will be the beginning of better days."

"Well I hope to help you out as best as I can. I see you've grown up since I last saw you."

"I'm just tryin' to get money, Flaco. You're the one who looks like you been in that gym."

Flaco had picked up a few pounds all in the right places. His chest stuck out more, his arms had become bigger, and his face had gotten more toned.

"Yes, you're right. I've learned that the tighter I keep my body, the less I have to pay for pretty young ladies.

As they laughed at Flaco's retort the waitress returned.

"Aqui estas tragos." she said placing their drinks on the table.

After getting tipped she hurried over to her next awaiting customer.

Turning up his double shot, and taking it down in one gulp, Jilla sat the glass down and folded his hands on the table. Getting straight to business, he looked Flaco in the eyes and told him what was on his mind.

"What's up, Flaco? I'm here now. When I get through dumping the rest of this order I got now, I'm trying to fuck wit' you. You remember how Great was taking care of the business for you? Well I'm doing double that in less the time."

"I see." Flaco said nodding his head up and down in approval.

"Da dude I been fuckin' wit, he ain't loyal Flaco. It seems like the more money I bring him, da higher he raise da prices on me. And his shit been getting weaker and weaker every batch lately."

"How much Jilla?

"Like eighteen-five or nineteen."

"No how much can you move?"

"I'm movin' 20 keys or better a week if da shit is good."

"Have you ever known me not to have good shit?"

"No, that's why I wanna fuck with you."

"Do you have a team?"

"Yeah, me, Demon, and Ugly got the whole East-Side sewed up. Everybody buy dey shit from us. Oh yeah, you got a hookup on dat hydro?"

"Yes, mi primo messes with that. Can you move that too?"

"Yeah. Red, Strawberry, and Passion got a nice clientele on dat. Fuck wit' us Flaco and you won't regret it."

I bet I won't, Flaco thought to himself. "Okay, tell me how much and when you'll be ready."

"I'll tell you what, give me a couple of days to dump the rest of what I got now. After I'm done I'mma call yo' phone and let you know what da order gone be. It's to the sky from here, Flaco. You know I ain't gone let you down." Jilla then held up his beer to Flaco, proposing a toast, "To da future."

"To da future" Flaco repeated tapping his glass to Jilla's beer bottle.

Looking at his Movado he noticed that it was time for him to handle his next order of business."

"Aight Flaco, I gotta get up outta here business awaits." Jilla said cocking his head to the side, sporting a smile. He stood up and extended his hand to Flaco for a shake.

"I'll speak with you soon." Flaco said shaking Jilla's hand

and using his free hand to pat him on the shoulder.

Jilla made his way out of the lounge and hopped in his rental. It was time to meet up with the rest of the crew so that they could execute a power move.

* * * *

Sitting in the living room of Dee's grandmother's house Jilla thought back to the days when she used to live down the block from him. Looking at her all tied down in her favorite rocking chair made him feel kind of bad. Nothing personal, strictly business he told himself to soothe his conscious. Growing tired of looking at her, he went into the kitchen where Demon, Passion and Ugly were.

"Wut up fool?" Ugly said dumping the tobacco out of a blunt wrap.

"Shit my nigga, just waitin' on dis chump to come in. I know somebody done called him for somethin'. Jilla responded as he lifted the ski-mask up off his face and sat down at the table. Dee's grandmother seeing his face probably would 've made her have a stroke right then and there.

"Here he come." Red ran into the kitchen and said. Jilla slid his mask back down over his face and everyone took their positions.

"Granny." Dee shouted as he walked into the house, He had three gym bags with him. One in each hand and one on his shoulder.

Shutting the door with his foot, then sitting one of the gym bags down, he locked the front door.

Cliickk.

"Bitch don't move." Demon calmly whispered pressing his gun against the back of Dee's neck. "What the-"

THUMP!

Demon smacked Dee upside his head. Strawberry then began searching him to make sure he didn't have a gun on him.

"Sit him right there." Jilla instructed, pointing to the armchair that he had placed right next to his Grandmother's rocking chair.

Placing Dee inside the chair, Ugly taped him to it by his wrist and ankles. With all of the curtains and blinds now shut, Jilla raised his mask exposing his face.

"Jilla!" Dee's Grandmother blurted out.

"Dis wut you on lil nigga? Dee added.

"Nigga I want everything right mufuckin now. Every single penny you own I want it. Where it at?"

"Jilla!!" Dee's Grandmother shouted again.

"Miss Campbell dis ain't got nothin' to do wit' you. Dee know what dis is all about."

"Wut you talkin' bout lil nigga."

"Why you ain't been answering my mufuckin' calls?"

"Ain't shit been happenin."

"Yeah, wut deez bags fo' den?" Jilla replied walking over to the duffel bags that Dee brought in the house with him.

Unzipping them one by one, they all were filled with money.

"Dat's some shit a mufucker owed me." Dee pled.

"Naw nigga, you wasn't answerin' my call cause you was too busy fuckin' my bitch behind my back."

Dee's eyes widened. "Wut da fuck you talkin' bout lil nigga."

"Dis, pussy mufucker." Jilla un-clipped his phone, flipped it open and pointed to the picture of Dee and Camelle in his face just as he did Camelle. Dee was at a loss for words.

"Come on wit dat shit." Jilla continued snapping his fingers twice. Red and Passion came out of the kitchen with two containers of gasoline.

Grabbing a container out of Passion's hand, Jilla began pouring gas all over Miss Campbell. "Jilla, boy you done gone crazy."

As Jilla did that, Red doused Dee with gas as well. Pulling a Zippo lighter out of his pocket, Ugly flicked it on.

"You and yo' Granny's life or da wealth? Which one is it?" Jilla propositioned.

"Boy you better give 'em what dey want." Miss Campbell cried out. The fumes from the gas were beginning to make her feel nauseous.

"Okay! Okay!" Dee shouted out. "It's in the basement."

"Demon, untie him and y'all take this disloyal ass nigga to da basement. If he makes one funny lookin' move, don't hesitate to knock his mufuckin' noodles back."

Ugly, Demon, Passion and Strawberry took Dee to the basement. As Red stood look out, at the living room window, Miss Campbell just looked at Jilla with pleading eyes. He ignored her silent solicitation. Money was the only thing capable of healing the wound caused by Dee and Camelle's disloyalty towards him. "Nigga we hit da lotto." Demon said, as he emerged from the basement with two bags in his hand. Passion and Strawberry were behind him with two bags as well. Ugly guided Dee, holding the back of his collar, while poking him in the head with his pistol.

It's gone take us at least three more trips but let's tie dis bitch-made mufucker back down first." said Ugly.

They gagged and bound Dee again, only this time handcuffing him to the cast-ironed radiator, and then proceeding to empty out the safe. Once done, they gathered up everything and began loading it into the cars.

Mmmf, mmmf, mmm, Dee pled with muffled cries.

After glancing around to make sure they hadn't forgotten anything, Jilla walked up to Dee and snatched the tape off of his mouth.

"Dat was some expensive ass pussy wasn't it?" Jilla asked, pulling out his pistol.

"You got what you wanted now just let us go," Dee demanded.

"Fuck dat! You betrayed us!" Jilla shouted.

As Ms. Campbell sat, bound in the rocking chair, her eyes were closed, and she was looking up to the sky as if she was praying. Jilla raised his Glock and sent rounds into her chest BLACOW! BLACOW! BLACOW! The impact of the .40 cal flipped her and the chair over backwards.

"What da fuck is you doin? I gave you what you wanted!" Dee began to shout hysterically.

Picking up the container of gasoline again, Jilla walked over to Dee and poured the rest of the gas over his head.

"Come on nigga, hurry up." Ugly said, reentering the house.

"Let's get the fuck outta here."

"Let me see dat lighter." Jilla asked him.

Ugly reached in his pocket, grabbed the lighter and tossed it across the room to were Jilla was.

"Don't nothing come close to a cross but a double cross," Jilla said through clenched teeth. The thickness of his vein running down his forehead let Dee know that his life was about to end.

Tossing the lighter onto his lap, Dee's entire body erupted into a ball of fire. Hearing his screams of torment and watching his body burn to a crisp, numbed the pain that Dee's acts had caused him. Cutting it close, Jilla snapped out of the daze he was in and ran to the car.

CHAPTER TWENTY-SIX

"Heeyy y'all!!" greeted Michelle as Demon and Jilla entered the back door of her apartment.

Sitting down the two big boxes wrapped with bright blue bows, both of them began to make their way over to the couch. Scanning the room, they took in the faces of all in sight. Satisfied that they were somewhat familiar, they took off their coats and had a seat.

What many people would view as paranoia, Jilla and Demon saw it as caution. Things had tightened up and with the Feds on their trail, they felt as if their days were numbered and every move they made had to be calculated.

Normally, they wouldn't have even entertained the thought of being in the street on the East Side before the sun went down. Things had resorted to the night life or nothing, when it came to riding through the city. Less peculiar faces and more hiding places was now one of the rules that they were playing by.

"Look at your fat ass. You know I couldn't miss my Sis's

baby shower." Demon said as he rubbed on Michelle's stomach. "You know he gone be a gangsta when he grow up don't you? He got my blood in him. His daddy ain't no chump, is he?"

"Yeah, as a matter of fact, where his daddy at? We need to check him out." Jilla cut in.

"Boy shut up. He ain't even here. But I got something for you." Michelle replied to Jilla.

"What you mean he ain't here? When he coming?" Jilla asked looking around the living room. "And what you mean you got something for me? I hope it's some money." he joked.

"Like I said, he ain't..." Michelle began to say as phone vibrated and interrupted her. Pausing, she hurriedly answered the phone. After putting it to her ear, and pressing another button, a smile formed across her face.

"Hey baby."

"Baby??? Oh, dat's da nigga right there? Tell him he need to be making it over here so niggaz can holla at him. I'm trying to see who main man is." Demon demanded.

"Here then." Michelle said as she shoved the phone into Demon's chest and wobbled towards the kitchen where the rest of her friends were.

"Hello!!" Demon spat into the phone as Jilla picked up the remote control and began surfing through the T.V. channels to try and catch the W.G.N. news.

"Colors!! Aw naw nigga, say it ain't so."

Hitting the mute button on the T.V., Jilla immediately looked over at Demon. Hearing Colors name seized his full attention and reminded him just how much he missed his nigga who had been with him since the beginning; the days when they were spot workers for Great. There was nothing that him, Colors and Dusty hadn't done together. Robbed, stole, sexed down girls, any and everything else imaginable, they'd done together.

Content, because they were on Michelle's phone, Jilla hollered at Colors, after Demon had done so himself. After Demon got done talking to Colors, he handed the phone to Jilla. Cause they were own Michelle's phone instead of their own, Jilla talked to Colors for only a few minutes. As he did, he looked over at Demon and could tell that he was feeling a certain type of' way after learning that his sister had been impregnated by Colors. After a few, *is you straight* and *don't trip, you gone beat dat shits*, the phone beeped signaling that Colors' phone time was about to expire.

"Aight fool, the phone finna hang up." Colors said sounding sad. Jilla took the sadness in Colors voice as a show of how much he missed his niggaz and his freedom.

"Aight boy. Niggaz miss you out here in deez streets too. Don't trip tho. Yo' boy got da street side of dis shit locked. Da night after yo' trial the whole team gone pop bottles fool. Hold ya head up my nigga."

After that was said the whole phone went dead. Hitting the end button, Jilla snapped the phone shut. Attempting to hand it to Demon, he caught him in deep thought.

Colors and Michelle had been creeping around ever since they were teenagers. Afraid of how Demon would take it, and not wanting to cause any ill will, Michelle and Colors both had decided that it would be best to keep their little tryst to themselves. But now that she was pregnant, the truth had to come to the light.

Demon wasn't feeling his sister being pregnant by one of his team members, not one bit. He tried not to let Jilla see it though, but it was too late. Demon knew how tight the bond was between Jilla and Colors, plus he didn't want to seem like he was on no soft shit. Jilla on the other hand, he just hoped his other main man, Demon, could just eventually get over it with no love lost. He just wouldn't speak on it.

"Where he go? He gone?" Michelle questioned as she wobbled back into the living room with her left hand resting on top of her belly. Biting down on the right side of her bottom lip and squinching her eyes, she tried to get a read out of her brother's facial expression.

As Jilla handed Michelle her phone, her and Demon's eyes locked sending and receiving a silent sibling to sibling message to one another.

Blowing off Demon's piercing stare, Michell turned to Jilla. "You ready for what I got for you?"

Happy to try to ease the building up tension, Jilla responded. "You got that bankroll for me?"

Making her way to where Jilla was seated, she placed her hands over his eyes. "It's a surprise. Stand up and follow my lead." *We done had enough surprises for today*, Jilla thought to himself.'

Entering the kitchen, Jilla smelled the mixed sent of various perfumes. When Michelle uncovered his eyes the sight before him sent him into complete awe.

Destiny stood in front of him living up to the term, *flawless*, in every shape and fashion. Her 34-25-40 frame left him astonished to the point that he found his usually conversational savvy self at a loss for words. It had been a couple of years since he'd seen her and she'd filled out a lot, in that time.

"You gone say something?" Michelle blurted out as the other women could be heard letting out slight chuckles.

Destiny just stood there with her left fingernail pressed up against her bottom lip satisfied with the reaction she was getting from Jilla. She knew she was fine. Guys tried to come at her everywhere she went but she always used her consumption with her schooling as the reason not to take any of them seriously.

"Aw naw," Jilla said as he eyed Destiny up and down with his head cocked to the side and an auspicious smile on his face. "It just take a little time to take in all this beauty that's right here before me."

CHAPTER TWENTY-SEVEN

2 MONTHS LATER

Exiting the expressway, Red looked at her rearview mirror. She was coming from picking up the 50 pounds of dro' that had been left in a vehicle that Flaco's Uncle left for her in the parking lot of the Ford City Mall. After Jilla and Demon had left from Michelle's baby shower they went and met up with Flaco to discuss business.

The gold minivan driven by an inconspicuous Caucasian looking woman was considered to be a good way to move when it came to transporting drugs. Due to being on the run, the *Bar None* Crew purchased houses spread throughout the suburbs surrounding Chicago.

Red had bought a house for her, Passion, and Strawberry out in Romeoville, Illinois, and this is where she was headed. As she reached the block that they lived on, she checked her rearview again to make sure that she wasn't being followed. Looking down from the rearview mirror and ahead of her, she had to slam on her brakes.

"Shit!!!" she yelled to herself as she hit the button lowering the driver's side window. "Sorry 'bout that." she pled to the man that was crossing the road carrying a weed-whacker in his hand. It was one of the workers from the lawn service that was tending to her neighbor's yard.

Surprisingly he remained calm, seeing how close she had come to hitting him. He replied in a polite manner.

"No problem ma'am."

Feeling a little bit guilty and knowing that she would be needing a company herself to tend to the three acres of land surrounding her house, she asked him if he would happen to have a business card on hand.

"No ma'am, we just gave the last one to a gentleman who passed by about three minutes ago." The landscaper replied. "But if you give me the address to the place that you need us to take care of, we'll be more than glad to come by and give you a free estimate."

"Well this is it right next door." Red replied pointing to her house.

"Oh okay, well that's no problem." the man replied acknowledging her house. "We've got a busy schedule today, but how about we come back tomorrow? If you're not home, we'll drop our brochure along with the estimate in your mailbox, and you can just give us a call if you would like our services?"

"That sounds like a plan." Red replied. "And sorry again for almost hitting you."

"NO problem, as long as it was almost." the man said with a smile. "Have a nice day ma'am." He nodded before heading over to the rest of his crew who were busy at work. After checking her rearview mirror once again, Red looked ahead, this time before taking her foot off the brake. Pulling into her driveway, she reached up at the sun visor for the garage-door opener forgetting that she had switched vehicles. Reaching in her purse she pulled out her cell phone and called Passion. "Open the garage and come on so y'all can help me with these bags." she said knowing her girls would know what she was referring to. Within seconds the garage door opened as Passion and Strawberry awaited inside.

Out of nowhere blurs of sirens and tires screeching came from all directions. "Freeze, get on the ground and keep your hands where we can see em, D. E. A.!"

All of the men that had been working on the neighbor's yard now had badges out and guns aimed at them.

* * * *

Aside from a condo on the north side, Jilla bought another house as well. Only this one was in Elgin, Illinois and he put it in Destiny's name.

The house was convenient for both Jilla and Destiny. It was close enough to school for Destiny, who was attending Northwestern University. And it wasn't too far of a drive for Jilla to get back and forth from the city.

Ever since Jilla ran back into Destiny at Michelle's baby shower, he'd gradually been spending more and more time with her, which eventually led to purchasing the current habitat that the two of them now shared as a home. Even though, after Camelle's act of disloyalty, Jilla told himself that he'd never get deep off into another women, things were different with Destiny.

Sitting up on the living room sofa, Jilla attentively watched the T.V. as the Bears quarterback threw an interception which resorted in a touchdown run back for the Minnesota Vikings.

"Fuck!!!" He pouted as he slammed his fist into the seat of the couch. He had a $10,000 bet on the Bears.

Looking at the scoreboard, reconfirming what he already knew, the Bears were now down three points. With two minutes and thirty-seven seconds left, his cell phone vibrated on the living room table in front of him. Picking it up and looking at the screen he was surprised to see that it was his attorney's office calling on a Sunday.

"Hello."

"Hey it's me, Roy." the attorney that Jilla hired to work on everyone's cases. Roy spoke into the phone in a sort of high-strung manner. "I got some bad news."

After informing Jilla on what had happened with his female cohorts, all that he could do was hang his head. As he did that, Jilla heard the sports announcer blurt from the T.V. *Vikings hold onto win 27-24.*"

* * * *

The next morning it was business as usual. Jilla had a nice place of ground to make up due to the loss of the 50 pounds of 'dro. Not to mention the money the Bears had lost him.

As they sat and ate their breakfast at the House of Pancakes in Homewood, Illinois, Jilla filled Demon and Ugly in on everything that the attorney had told him. Seeming to be in a state of somberness, they all basically just picked over their food. Things were getting tight, and like a game of chess, every move that each of them made, counted detrimentally. Informing them that he was on his way to the attorney's office, Jilla waived the waitress over so that he could get the tab.

"I'mma jump in the car with you." Demon said as he stood up to put on his coat.

"Nah, I need you and Ugly to gone and work ya'll magic with the rest of this work we got left. We gotta get back killa, and duck these Alphabet Boys. Plus I gotta go holla at Flaco, and you know how he get when I get to bringin' mufuckers around him. As soon as I get done I'mma hit y'all phones so we can all link back up."

An apparent show of disapproval formed on Demon's face as they all exited the restaurant, but once Jilla said he was going to get up with Flaco he knew the procedure. "Aight fool. Be careful my nigga, we the last three left. We gotta stay free til all this shit's over."

Ugly just remained quiet as usual. The wheels in his head were turning a million times a second.

Jilla jumped in his rental and Demon and Ugly jumped in the rental they were driving. As they exited the parking lot, they threw the *Bar None* sign up to each other going their separate ways.

* * * *

Sitting inside the Law office of Nelson and Blakely, Jilla was heated. The long-awaited *discovery* in Colors and Dusty's arrest had finally been disclosed. The conference room had an assortment of attorneys from the firm sitting in on the meeting because they wanted to make sure that nothing was missed from any angle. As they collectively sifted through the paperwork, the room was silent.

It was at this moment and time, from reading through all of the papers, that Jilla realized where all of the heat on the *Bar None* crew had come from. *Muthafuckin' Colors*, he mouthed to himself.

"Excuse me." Roy said while using his index finger to push his glasses up higher on the bridge of his nose.

"Nah, I'm just sayin'. From reading this, if Colors never started messing with this nigga Dimp, none of this shit would ever be going on." The part that hurt Jilla even worse was who the informant was. Everybody knew Dimp was a snitch. And Jilla knew that Colors did as well.

"Yeah, if you're referring to the transaction between Mr. Dunston and the informant that seems to be the case."

Bar None was built from the ground up; a family of go-getting killers who did and would do anything to aid and assist the well-being, and betterment, of each other. They played by certain rules and mingling with snitches was completely against them. Snitches were non-conducive to what they did and just plain bad news. When someone veered away from the rules, they subjected themselves to being declared an enemy of the clique and were dealt with in that fashion. Not only did they go by the name *Bar None*, they also carried themselves in a *Bar None* fashion as well.

"So what dis shit mean?" Jilla asked as he sunk back in the

chair he was sitting in.

Mr. Blakely cleared his throat as he fidgeted with the Etoile de Montblanc ink pen. "Well this informant guy is going to get on the stand and it is going to be our job..." he gestured pointing at the three other attorneys "to discredit and jam the prick up in some lies."

"Yes, because he's the entire case." one of the other attorneys interjected. "Him and this Gomez chick that was with Duston. She's talking too."

"So what about the girls? They got a bond?" Jilla queried.

"Just like the guy, they won't get a bond due to the seriousness of the case." Roy said. "It'll be a while as well, before we get their discovery. You know it's always a waiting game with the fucking Feds. They try to keep you in those jails as long as possible, hoping you'll turn informant. But I am curious as to how they're tying everyone else into this to make it a conspiracy. Someone else is definitely talking."

Elbows planted on the table, Jilla lowered his head and began rubbing it. Knowing that he had a task ahead of him he stood and reached inside both of his pockets pulling out two rubber banned knots of money. "Thanks." he said throwing them on the table in front of him. "Keep me posted and make sure you go let the girls know what's going on. Roy." Shutting the office door behind him. Jilla headed to his car.

* * * *

After leaving the attorneys office Jilla had a couple of hours before it was time to meet up with Flaco. He decided to run to Border's bookstore so that he could purchase some books and magazines for the girls, Dusty, and Colors. From there, he went to the Currency Exchange and got money orders for them as well.

As he stood at the counter inside of the post office filling every one's names out on the flat rate envelopes, he drifted off in thought as he got to the last one for Colors'.

I shouldn't send this nigga shit, he thought to himself.

"Excuse me sir you ready?" asked the salt & pepper headed older lady, who was the window clerk snapping Jilla out of his thoughts.

"Oh, sorry about that." Jilla said pushing all of the envelopes through the window. Retrieving his receipt, he exited the Post Office.

Colors had been on Jilla's mind. Every since he'd learned where all of the heat on the crew had evolved from. He knew that Colors dealing with Dimp was a direct result of the headlock that the casino had him in.

He thought about how any habit; whether it be drugs, gambling, or whatever else, could cause an individual to resort to things that they knew better than to resort to.

However, the fact remained that Colors, the same nigga that Jilla first hit the block with, his right-hand man, had put the entire crew's lives and freedom in jeopardy, because he started fucking with a snitch.

CHAPTER TWENTY-EIGHT

In the back of an automobile window tinting shop, Jilla sat in front of the desk that Flaco was seated behind. The room was quiet and Flaco could noticeably see that Jilla wasn't his usual self.

"What's going on Jilla? You seem troubled." Flaco pried as he poured the Deleon Tequila into his glass.

Taking a sip, he sat the glass back on the desk and cleared his throat awaiting Jilla's response.

"Maaan, shit just been all fucked up." Jilla responded.

Looking keenly into Jilla's eyes, Flaco scooted his chair up closer to the desk, placed his elbows on it, and folded his hands in front of him. "What exactly is fucked up my friend?"

Jilla filled him in on what had happened with the girls and what he had found out about Colors.

"SO let me get this right. You informed the girls on where to pick the Hydro Marijuana up at. They picked it up, went to where you told them to take it to. And the cops were there waiting on them?"

"Yup"

"And you say this Colors guy is the beginning of all of this

"Yeah"

"But none of the 40 kilograms of coke that I sold to you got hemmed up in this?"

"Nah, as a matter of fact, I'll be ready for you in a couple more days."

"Okay, I see."

Finishing the rest of his drink. Flaco untopped the bottle of Tequila and refilled his glass, this time gesturing an offer of some.

"Nah, I'm cool." Jilla responded.

"So where does this leave us Jilla?" Flaco asked while tracing his finger around the rim of his glass. "You know, our business?"

"Man Flaco, I got some making up to do. You know I gotta still straighten out your Primo for the 'dro. I gotta keep my face clean. So we still good. As a matter of fact, we probably gooder. I'm trying to move about 50 keys a week now. I ain't wit takin losses."

Just as Jilla finished selling his hustle, the phone on top of the desk rang. Giving Jilla a gesture by finger to wait a second, Flaco answered. After listening to a few words spoken by whoever was on the other end, Flaco responded with an, "Okay." and hung up.

"All right Jilla. So you have things under control?" Flaco asked while standing at the same time.

"No question!' Jilla assured him.

"Well I'll see you in a couple of days. Just call me when you're ready." Flaco reached his hand out to Jilla for a shake.

"Got another business matter to tend to."

"Aight, a couple of days then." Jilla reassured as he and Flaco shook.

* * * *

A couple of weeks later, after leaving River Oaks Mall, from shopping, Jilla turned down the block next to Destiny's Mother's house. She had talked him into riding through the hood, something that he definitely wasn't feeling, so that she could pick up the stack of mail that her mother informed her had built up over her house.

The street was packed with cars.

Honk! Honk!!

Jilla impatiently sounded off his horn, breaking Destiny out of the daze that the Macy's dressing room sex they'd just had left her in.

Looking over at the driver's seat, she could see Jilla's eyes transfixed on someone, displaying nothing but malice. Turning her attention toward the direction he was looking in; she noticed the familiar face of one of her old grammar school classmates. He was greeting an elderly lady, who'd just stepped out of a Cadillac Eldorado, with a hug.

"Is that Dimp?" Destiny blurted out, not believing her eyes. She knew the involvement Dimp had in Dusty and Colors being locked up and she had already known he'd gotten locked up from listening to Michelle gossip.

"Yeah, I got dis bitch ass nigga." Jilla replied scooting down lower into his seat as if someone could spot him behind the deep dark tint that covered the windows of the Pontiac Grand Prix GTS.

Immediately grabbing the .40 caliber Glock off of his lap, the death grip that his right hand had on it was met hastily with Destiny's left hand.

"Unh, Unh, boy. You ain't finna do nothing stupid while I'm in this car with you. Look at you, you ain't got no mask on or nothin'. Don't you see all these witnesses out here? It look like they havin' a family reunion or somethin'! Do you think they'll hesitate to come and point your ass out in court? Especially about doin' something to their own family member. I ain't tryin' to lose you like that Jilla. In case you didn't know, I love you."

Realizing that the words Destiny had just spoken were true, Jilla loosened the grip of his .40 cal. and sat it back down on his lap. As long as he'd been playing the murder game, he'd never thought about pulling the trigger before he did it. Things just went down spur of the moment and fortunately for him he had never had to pay the consequences. Destiny may have very well saved him from that suffering at this very moment.

Slowly weaving through the rest of the cars on the block, Jilla turned the corner and pulled into Destiny's mother's driveway.

"Just get your mother's car and drive home. We'll bring it back in the mornin'."

As much as Destiny hated to, she had to let Jilla do what she knew he had to do to secure his and his guy's freedom. "Be careful." she said as she opened the door to get out of the car.

"You better come straight home too."

After kissing him on the cheek she got out of the car and shut the door behind her.

After making sure Destiny got into the house safe, Jilla sped. off while punching numbers into his cell phone. It was time to put in work.

* * * *

"Mail call! Shouted the husky, man-looking female guard, as she stood in the middle of the day-room common area. "Paul Madison, Kenyatta Smith, Lori Roberts, Sophi Gomez.

The guard yelled out name after name until the stack of mail that sat on the table in front of her was gone. One of the women's name stood out to Red, as she walked away with her package, and froze her dead in her tracks. She knew she hadn't heard what she thought she did, but the reality of the matter was she did.

Her, Passion, and Strawberry were all housed at the M.C.C. building in downtown Chicago. Conveniently for them, they all resided on the same unit. Even though they were no longer free, they still had each other. That alone made their predicament better for them.

While there, they had to set a few examples on some of the other female inmates letting them know that they weren't to be taken lightly. After the message got across, from a few bloody encounters, the rest of the women kept it respectable and stayed out of their way.

"Girl snap out of it." Strawberry said as she sat back down

at the table where her, Red, and Passion had been playing cards at. "Hoe don't let me find out you on some homesick shit today."

Grabbing her favorite, sister 2 sister, out of the stack, Red opened it and used it to cover her mouth. "The bitch that's telling on Colors is on this unit."

Passion almost choked on the sip of Pepsi that she had just taken and immediately began scanning the dayroom. "Where the bitch at?" she mumbled without moving her lips.

"Don't even trip. We just gone go to our cell one by one, so we don't look suspicious." Red replied, "It's curtains for that bitch."

* * * *

"It's all types of mufuckaz up in here, old people and all." Lil Gadi whispered to Ugly as they knelt down peeping into the kitchen window of Dimp's mother's house from the backyard.

After Jilla dropped Destiny off, the first person he called was Demon. But after calling seven straight times, back to back, getting nothing but his voice mail, he called Ugly who told him that he hadn't heard from Demon all that day. Figuring that Demon was somewhere fucking off with some chick, he just told Ugly to meet up with him and bring the shorties.

"Man Shorty, ain't no mercy on no snitches. Dey get they self and every mufucka dat's close to em' killed for fucking wit' niggaz like us." Ugly replied in a low tone as he clutched the automatic AK-47 he had resting on his knee.

Lil Gadi and Illa ended up getting their drug cases thrown

out due to an S.O.L. technicality of their names not being on the lease of the spot. Not even a full week into being free, it was time to put in that work.

As Ugly jogged back to the alley, Jilla and Illa were in the front of the house setting up their positions as well. Posted up in-between the two houses directly adjacent to Dimp's mother's, the all black Dickie Suit and ski-mask left Jilla unnoticeable due to the darkness of the night.

Chirp... Chirp...

"Let's do it." Jilla's voice chimed through the speaker of Ugly's Nextel.

"It's on." Ugly replied.

Simultaneously, they both gave the signal to Illa and Gadi by flashing the miniature flashlights they had twice.

Flicking the cigarette lighter on, Gadi lit the torn string of cloth that was hanging out of the 40 oz. bottle filled with gasoline. In the front of the house, Lil Illa did the same thing.

CRASH!!! CRASH!!!

Was all that was heard as the bottles that were flung smashed through the windows. Illa and Gadi took off running to the car.

All Jilla and Demon saw were gigantic balls of fire erupting inside the house. Then it was their turn.

DACK! ! ! DACK! ! ! DACK! ! ! DACK! ! !
BLACOW! ! ! BLACOW! ! ! BLACOW! ! !

Automatic gunfire was all that was heard. As people attempted to exit the house fire they were greeted with a barrage of hot steel, at the front and back doors, ripping through their flesh.

CHAPTER TWENTY-NINE

"A Colors, my new celly say he from yo' hood." One of the guys from over east, named Big D, shouted down from the top tier.

Giving Big D a nod, and them glancing up at who he was referring to, Colors continued on with the conversation he was having with Michelle. She was filling him in on the details of what she'd read in the newspaper about what had happened to Dimp and his family. As he listened, Colors was all smiles, thinking about how he was one more step closer to freedom.

The beep sounded signaling that the call was about to come to an end. "You coming to visit me tomorrow?" Colors asked as the phone cut off. Unable to get an answer he got up and placed the phone in the cradle.

Tucking the newspaper under his arm, Colors jogged up the stairs to Big D 's cell. When he made it to the room, the new guy was making up his bunk. *Damn dis nigga swole as hell* Colors thought to himself. "Where you from Big Homie?"

"I'm from da Manor, Whassup?"

"My name is Colors. I'm from da Manor too. *Bar None.*"

Colors boasted, knowing the type of weight *Bar None* carried.

Looking Colors up and down, as he reached his hand out for a pound. Big Dude honed in on the *Bar None* tattoo Colors had on his forearm. "You *Bar None*, huh?"

"To da grave." Colors retorted.

Feeling a bit more comfortable, the Big Dude bumped fist with Colors completing the pound. "My names Quick Draw."

"Quick Draw!!! Dey call you Q.D.?"

"Yeah dat's me."

"I used to hear Great, Luke, and Rello talkin' 'bout you all da time."

"Dem was my niggaz, dey was all a mufucka had. I been hearin… about you young fools too. Still representin'. I see my niggaz groomed some true go-getters.

"Ain't no question fool. You know how we do, *Bar None* or nothing."

After doing a little more bonding. Colors filled Q. D. in on the indictment that the *Bar None* crew was facing. Q. D. had already known everything that Colors told him, but he listened to everything he said attentively.

Once done with the filling in, Colors had Nickel Slick go get Q. D. a care package: 4 bags full of commissary, 2 knives, 2 jogging suits, 2 pair of gym shoes, a radio, and an ounce of weed. Later, they found themselves inside of Colors' cell.

"So what's going on with yo' shit?"

"I got court coming up to see if dey gone give me some action on my appeal. I'm tryin' to give this life sentence back so a nigga can get back out there and fuck some of dem pretty ass model bitches I been seeing on dem B.E.T. videos."

"Shiitt, I hope all of us can touch back down cuz we got

plenty of bitches my nigga." Colors said as he sat up and grabbed the newspaper off of the desk. "Fool and em' tryin' to make it happen." He finished, tossing the paper into Q.D.'s lap' After reading the front page, Q. D. began nodding his head up and down, "That's whassup!"

* * * *

Sitting inside of Jilla's North-Side condo, Flaco let him know about how things had to go a bit differently in the way they conducted business due to him relocating to another state.

"So you telling me I'mma be dealing with some other mufuckaz." Jilla asked.

"There's no choice Jilla, unless you want to come to Texas to get it. I'm having it delivered to you, and at a cheaper price. You'll make an extra point off of each key. You get 40 keys from me a week so that'll add up to an extra forty-thousand dollars."

Weighing his options, Jilla went along with it. Flaco had been a major factor in the money that he was now seeing. Plus, he figured that this would help him with his plan all the more.

"Aight Flaco, It's all good. After all, it's about progress, right? Jilla said and flashed his signature smile.

"Exactó." Flaco responded.

* * * *

Sitting inside of their cell, Red, Strawberry, and Passion were plotting on how the business was to be addressed. Despite the fact that they didn't mingle with the other women on the unit too tough, they'd taken a liking to this one chick.

She was a pretty mulatto woman, with the exact same complexion as Red. Going down the side of her face, a tattoo of the letters S. I. C. K, adorned her right cheek. This was how she got her name. With average size breast, she had a thin waist and a bubble shaped booty. Standing about 5'6", her legs complemented her body perfectly. She wore her hair naturally short and curly.

Sick wasn't from Chicago but had gotten pulled over for speeding on the Dan Ryan Expressway while in route to Miami going to visit her grandmother in the hospital. Looking at the tattoo on her face the State Troopers became suspicious and searched the vehicle. In the trunk, up under the spare tire, they found a 9-millimeter handgun. Knowing the gun belonged to one of her homegirls, whom the car belonged to, Sick stayed true to the game and kept her mouth shut.

Due to her extensive criminal background, the ATF picked up her case. When the prosecutor sent word to her through her attorney, suggesting that she cooperate or take a plea bargain, she adamantly sent word back that it was trial or nothing. Facing 30 to life, Sick was a real street bitch, and Red instantly took a liking to her.

Sick had exhibited all of the qualities of a *real bitch* so far, and today was the day that she'd show if she was officially *Bar None* material or not. Getting up from her seat in the dayroom where all of the other women were watching *Hustle-NF 2,* Maria, the Brazilian chick, got up and headed to her room. It was that time of the month and she had to change her tampon.

Entering her cell, Maria shut the door behind. She pulled down her pants, and sat down on the toilet stool. As she reached over inside of her locker, which was right beside the toilet, all she noticed was someone lunging toward her, followed by a piece of heavy hard steel crashing upside her head. Trying to get a glimpse of her attacker in-between the steady thrashing, all that she was able to see was her perpetrator clad with a mask made out of a pillowcase, a jail uniform, and a pair of gloves on.

Attempting to stand up in defense, Maria's vision had become impaired due to the blood gushing out of her and running down into her eyes. Sick just kept beating and beating her nonstop. As Maria made it to her feet, she tried to rush her attacker. Losing her balance, due to her pants still being around her ankles, Maria fell and all Sick heard was *SNAP*! ! !

Maria had fell and broke her neck on the sink. Immediately after the snap Maria's body fell to the floor, lifeless. Sick kicked her in the stomach and stomped her head into the concrete floor. Leaving the cell, undetected, she then went and got rid of all the evidence.

* * * *

"Get the fuck outta here." Jilla said to Roy. "This shit can't be true. Can they make up somethin' like dis'?"

"No, they can't. Falsifying government documents would cost them their jobs."

Finally able to find out who it was that was tying the whole *Bar None* crew together in the conspiracy, Jilla just couldn't believe it.

"Look, we're not supposed to be seeing any of this. A friend of mines from the D. A.'s office owed me a favor and here we are." Roy said referring to the file folder marked confidential.

"You need to cut off all ties with this Flaco guy, if any, immediately. From what my friend says, they could've been brought you in, but they wanted to build your quantity level so high that the judge wouldn't think about giving you anything less than life. It's like they've just been sitting back, sort of letting you hang yourself."

"I can' t believe this shit."

"Well you better. From what I hear, this Flaco guy got caught up in a big conspiracy himself and had started working on helping the D. E. A. build a case on some guy who went by the name of Great. This guy and the rest of his crew died, and I guess this is when you came in the picture."

Jilla couldn't believe everything that he was hearing. *All of this time and Flaco's a mufuckin' snitch*, he thought to himself. All of what he was now learning explained a lot now that he looked back. Why Flaco couldn't be found when he initially went to the restaurant to look for him. Why he looked so fit and gained so much muscle mass when he finally did see him. And why he had recently told him that he was moving to Texas.

"So where is this Flaco guy at now?" Jilla asked.

"He's downtown in the M.C.C. building."

"Okay, so now what Roy?"

"Well I must admit, things were looking extremely well due to the unfortunate, but timely, demise of the witness against you guys. But this Flaco guy, he's really all they need. Him plus all of the audio from the wires he wore."

Hearing that, Jilla knew what he had to do. *Find Flaco by any means necessary.*

* * * *

Leaned up against the bleachers in the gym, Q.D. patiently waited out his prey. The courts had denied his appeal and even though he didn't plan on getting caught for what he was about to do, if he did, it wouldn't matter because he already had a life sentence.

The championship game of the winter league basketball tournament had the gym packed. Team-G defeated Team-D 74-73 to take the win. As the inmates headed to the elevators for yard recall, a dude named six-nine engaged in a slam dunk contest with another dude by the name of too-tall.

As the dunks captivated the attention of the straggling inmates, Q. D. snatch his victim up by the collar and dragged him beneath the bleachers. In the same motion, Q. D. plunged the icepick shank in and out of Flaco's stomach repeatedly.

"'Yeah bitch, snitches get it when dey fuck wit gangstaz."

Flaco attempted to say something but the blood hemorrhaging out of his mouth only allowed a gurgling sound to escape.

After repeatedly stabbing him in his chest and neck, Q. D. dropped Flaco to the ground, switched into the extra outfit that he had stashed, and eased from under the bleachers undetected.

CHAPTER THIRTY

Jilla and Destiny sat across the table from one another at Grand Lux Restaurant in downtown Chicago. It was the evening of Destiny's graduation from college and he used it as the perfect opportunity to confide in her how he was ready to give the game up and start a family with her. His bankroll was sitting pretty, and her educational achievements pointed towards a promising future for the two of them.

As he paid the waitress for their order, Jilla felt his cell phone vibrate in his pocket. Looking at the caller I.D. he saw that it was Ron, his attorney.

"I got good news for you." Ron bragged after Jilla answered the phone. "All charges have been dropped on everyone and they'll all be getting released tonight."

"Get outta here!" Jilla said sounding excited.

"Yeah. Seems your guy Flaco tapped out last night and there's no more witnesses."

When Q.D. stabbed up Flaco, he didn't die instantly. He'd been on life support in critical condition, for the past two and a half weeks. So, this news was a relief to Jilla's ears.

"Okay Ron, that's what's up. What time can we go pick 'em up?"

"I'd say around nine tonight. I'll call down there and put the press on em' as soon as I hang up."

"I'm outta here then. I'll bring the rest of your money down to your office tomorrow. Or maybe the day after cuz you know we're going to party hardy tonight." Jilla said with a smile on his face.

"Will do. See you then."

Jilla hit the end button on his phone and let Destiny in on what he'd just been told. She then called her aunt, Dusty's mom, passing on the good news.

* * * *

Club Crowbar was packed to capacity, it had been quite some time since the entire *Bar None* crew was able to kick it together like the family they were. Jilla looked around the V. I.P. section at his folks; Red, Passion, and Strawberry held their drinks up in the air as they moved their bodies to the music, Demon and Ugly were in the ear of two chicks who Jilla knew they were trying to get in the panties of before the night was over. Dusty, who was now walking on a cane, even had a Jamaican chick who he was macking down. Colors, who Jilla had signaled over, bobbed his head to the music as he took a seat next to Jilla.

"What's up fool?" Jilla asked talking over the music.

"Freedom my nigga. Glad to be free." Colors replied.

"So what's up? You ready to get this money again?"

"You know I got a shorty now nigga? The baby gotta eat don't he?"

Looking straight ahead, Jilla didn't look Colors in the eyes while he spoke to him. The subject of Colors' newborn son, along with a lot of other factors made him hope that the next question he asked got answered correctly. "I know datz right my nigga, stomach can't help but to be growling, huh?" Nodding toward the bathroom, Jilla took a swig from the bottle of Kristal. "Dey got yo' favorite game going on in the bathroom. Dice game jumpin'. You want some bread so you can go in there and lay your shot down?"

"Do I???" Colors responded wide-eyedingly.

Right then and there Jilla knew that Colors hadn't learned anything. Gambling clouded his judgement and it was a habit he hadn't kicked. Even though he was done with the game, Jilla knew the rest of the *Bar None* crew wasn't. And with all of the love he had for Colors, he still couldn't allow him to put the rest of the crew's freedom in jeopardy again because of his addiction.

"Gone out there and look in the trunk of my car." Jilla said pointing the bottom of the Kristal bottle at a car key that was laying on the table in front of them. "Look in dat Louis Vuitton bag and grab you a few stacks so you can break dem lames my nigga."

Eager to get to the crap game, Colors grabbed the key and headed out the front door of the club.

* * * *

Walking up to the car, Colors pressed the trunk release button on the car key, but it didn't work. Pressing it again, and again, with no success he walked up to the car and slid the key into the trunk lock. As he attempted to turn it, the key didn't work either. Jiggling it a bit, he tried to turn it again.

Hearing two sets of light footsteps come up behind him, Colors tried to turn around.

BOOM!! BOOM!!

Two shots sounded off as they entered and exited Colors head causing him to immediately fall to the ground.

BLAAK! ! ! BLAAK! ! ! -BLAAK! ! !

Rang the other three shots that penetrated his head.

As Colors' dead body lay sprawled on the ground, Illa grabbed the key out of the keyhole of Jilla's trunk and took off behind Gadi.

As much as Jilla hated to make the call, he had to do what he had to do. *Bar None*

Order Form

Contact Us: Contact@11Empireinc.com

Name:_____

Address:_____

City:_____ State:_____ Zip:_____

Amount		Book Title or Pen Pal Number	Price
		Included for shipping for 1 book	**$4 U.S. / $9 Inter**

This book can also be purchased on:
AMAZON.COM/ BARNES&NOBLE.COM

We Help You Self-Publish Your Book

You're The Publisher And We're Your Legs.
We Offer Editing For An Extra Fee, and Highly
Suggest It, If Waved, We Print What You Submit!

Crystell Publications is not your publisher, but we will help you self-publish your own novel.

Don't have all your money? .... No Problem!
Ask About our Payment Plans
Crystal Perkins-Stell, MHR
Essence Magazine Bestseller
We Give You Books!
PO BOX 8044 / Edmond – OK 73083
www.crystalstell.com
(405) 414-3991

Plan 1-A 190 - 250 pgs $719.00   **Plan 1-B 150 -180 pgs $674.00**

Plan 1-C 70 - 145pgs $625.00

2 (Publisher/Printer) Proofs, Correspondence, 3 books, Manuscript Scan and Conversion, Typeset, Masters, Custom Cover, ISBN, Promo in Mink, 2 issues of Mink Magazine, Consultation, POD uploads. 1 Week of E-blast to a reading population of over 5000 readers, book clubs, and bookstores, The Authors Guide to Understanding The POD, and writing Tips, and a review snippet along with a professional query letter will be sent to our top 4 distributors in an attempt to have your book shelved in their bookstores or distributed to potential book vendors. After the query is sent, if interested in your book, distributors will contact you or your outside rep to discuss shipment of books, and fees.

Plan 2-A 190 - 250 pgs $645.00   **Plan 2-B 150 -180 pgs $600.00**

Plan 2-C 70 - 145pgs $550.00

1 Printer Proof, Correspondence, 3 books, Manuscript Scan and Conversion, Typeset, Masters, Custom Cover, ISBN, Promo in Mink, 1 issue of Mink Magazine, Consultation, POD upload.

We're Changing The Game.

No more paying Vanity Presses $8 to $10 per book!

Made in the USA
Columbia, SC
16 September 2022

66911386R00143